A Word from Stephanie
About Cooking Up Trouble

I've just discovered a totally unknown talent—I'm a fabulous cook! Good enough to start my own catering business! And just in time too, because it's Uncle Jesse and Aunt Becky's anniversary. Everyone's getting them a special gift. Even the twins are creating a masterpiece (with some help from Michelle). So I'm cooking up a surprise of my own. All I need is some extra money—well, actually, lots of extra money. But with my cooking talent, earning cash will be no problem. I'm already swamped with catering jobs.

Then why does everyone think I need their help? Darcy and Allie don't believe I can boil an egg. My entire family is giving me advice. And I won't even mention what D.J. thinks of my ability to run a business! I can do it all. Except, lately, I'm having a few minor kitchen catastrophes.

Gulp! I hope this business wasn't another one of my half-baked ideas. While I'm waiting to find out, why don't I tell you about something that isn't a disaster—my family.

Right now there are nine people and a dog living in our house—and for all I know, someone new could move in at any time. There's me, my big sister, D.J., my little sister, Michelle, and my dad, Danny. But that's just the beginning.

D0291600

When my mom died, Dad needed help. So he asked his old college buddy, Joey Gladstone, and my uncle Jesse to come live with us, to help take care of me and my sisters.

Back then, Uncle Jesse didn't know much about taking care of three little girls. He was more into rock 'n' roll. Joey didn't know anything about kids, either—but it sure was funny watching him learn!

Having Uncle Jesse and Joey around was like having three dads instead of one! But then something even better happened—Uncle Jesse fell in love. He married Rebecca Donaldson, Dad's cohost on his TV show, *Wake Up, San Francisco*. Aunt Becky's so nice— she's more like a big sister than an aunt.

Next Uncle Jesse and Aunt Becky had twin baby boys. Their names are Nicky and Alex, and they are adorable!

I love being part of a big family. Still, things can get pretty crazy when you live in such a full house!

FULL HOUSE™: Stephanie novels

Available from MINSTREL Books

For orders other than by individual consumers, Pocket Books grants a discount on the purchase of **10 or more** copies of single titles for special markets or premium use. For further details, please write to the Vice-President of Special Markets, Pocket Books, 1633 Broadway, New York, NY 10019-6785, 8th Floor.

For information on how individual consumers can place orders, please write to Mail Order Department, Simon & Schuster Inc., 200 Old Tappan Road, Old Tappan, NJ 07675.

FULL HOUSE™
Stephanie

Sugar and Spice Advice

Devra Newberger Speregen

A Parachute Press Book

READING

A
MINSTREL®
BOOK

Published by POCKET BOOKS
New York   London   Toronto   Sydney   Tokyo   Singapore

The sale of this book without its cover is unauthorized. If you purchased this book without a cover, you should be aware that it was reported to the publisher as "unsold and destroyed." Neither the author nor the publisher has received payment for the sale of this "stripped book."

This book is a work of fiction. Names, characters, places and incidents are products of the author's imagination or are used fictitiously. Any resemblance to actual events or locales or persons, living or dead, is entirely coincidental.

A MINSTREL PAPERBACK *Original*

A Minstrel Book published by
POCKET BOOKS, a division of Simon & Schuster Inc.
1230 Avenue of the Americas, New York, NY 10020

A PARACHUTE PRESS BOOK

Copyright © and ™ 1996 by Warner Bros.

FULL HOUSE, characters, names and all related indicia are
trademarks of Warner Bros. © 1996.

All rights reserved, including the right to reproduce
this book or portions thereof in any form whatsoever.
For information address Pocket Books, 1230 Avenue
of the Americas, New York, NY 10020

ISBN: 0-671-56842-6

First Minstrel Books printing October 1996

10 9 8 7 6 5 4 3 2 1

A MINSTREL BOOK and colophon are registered trademarks of
Simon & Schuster Inc.

Cover photo by Schultz Photography

Printed in the U.S.A.

Sugar and Spice
Advice

CHAPTER

1

◆ ◀ ◾ ◆

"Hey! Cousin Stephanie, you're eating the cookie dough!" four-year-old Nicky Katsopolis shouted.

"You're supposed to *cook* it!" Alex, Nicky's twin brother, added.

Whoops! Busted! Stephanie Tanner swallowed the cookie dough. "Okay, guys, you caught me," she said. "Now you can have some too."

Nicky and Alex exchanged looks. "Really?" Nicky asked in excitement. Stephanie nodded.

"Yay!" Alex shouted.

Stephanie spooned more dough from the plastic wrapper. Nicky and Alex gobbled it up. Stephanie dropped more dough onto the cookie sheet. The night before, she'd promised to bake her cousins cookies to get them to put on their pajamas. It worked great. Nicky and Alex changed into pj's, brushed their teeth, and jumped into bed in five minutes flat!

Tonight she was keeping her promise. Luckily, Stephanie really liked baking cookies. Especially when the dough came ready-made from the supermarket.

She patted the dough into neat little mounds on the baking sheet and slipped the sheet into the oven. She set the oven timer for ten minutes.

"When the bell goes off, the cookies will be ready," she told Nicky and Alex.

The twins pulled a chair up in front of the oven window and sat down to watch the cookies bake. Stephanie chuckled. It was fun having little kids like Alex and Nicky around.

Stephanie's cousins lived upstairs, in the attic apartment. Their dad was Jesse Katsopolis, Stephanie's uncle. Uncle Jesse had come to live with the Tanner family eight years ago, after Stephanie's mother died in a car accident. Jesse helped Stephanie's father raise Stephanie and her two sisters. It was fun having an extra dad around. And even more fun when Jesse married Becky Donaldson and they had the twins.

Stephanie began cleaning off the kitchen counter.

Her older sister, D.J., stomped in through the back door.

"Hey, Deej! How was the library?" Stephanie asked.

D.J. dropped her backpack on the floor with a thud. She collapsed into a chair at the kitchen table.

"Awful," D.J. said. "If I have to spend one more second there, I'll go nuts!" D.J. groaned.

Stephanie couldn't believe how tired her sister looked. She knew college was a lot of work, but D.J. looked completely beat. "Too much school-work?" she asked.

D.J. glanced up wearily. "I've already used up two whole pens doing this week's assignments."

"Doesn't sound like much fun," Stephanie sympathized.

"It isn't. I can't take it anymore!" D.J. exclaimed. "The work never stops! But the worst is my econ class. There's a big presentation coming up soon."

Nicky made a face. "E-con?" he asked. "What's that?"

"She means economics," Stephanie explained. "That's the name of a college class."

Alex scrunched up his nose. "Don't you have finger-painting class, D.J.?"

"Don't I wish," she mumbled.

Stephanie sat down across from D.J. "So what's this big economics presentation about?" she asked.

D.J. frowned. "That's the problem," she explained. "I don't have a topic yet. And it's due in ten days."

Stephanie grimaced. "Yikes!" She paused. "Economics, that's about money, right? Hmmmmmm. I have an idea. What about a report on how they make money?" she suggested.

D.J. stared at her. "How *who* makes money?" she asked.

"I don't know," Stephanie replied. "That's what the report will be about. Who are the guys who make our money?"

D.J. shook her head. "No, no. That's not economics. Economics is more about *earning* money—like in business and stuff."

"Oh!" Stephanie said. "Then I guess you should write about somebody who owns a business."

"I don't know anyone who has their own business," D.J. replied.

Stephanie shrugged. "No problem. Why don't you just start a business yourself?" she asked.

D.J. snorted. "Sure! Start a business in ten days. Right. You make it sound easy. If you were older, like me, you'd realize that it's not!"

Stephanie bristled. "I bet I'm old enough to start

a business," she argued. "And I could use the money too," she went on. "Uncle Jesse and Aunt Becky's anniversary is coming up. I want to get them something special this year. Something—sophisticated."

D.J. stared at her. "If you need pocket money, ask Dad for an advance on your allowance."

"I already did," Stephanie admitted. "And I already spent it too."

"I guess you wish you never quit your job at the television station," D.J. remarked.

Stephanie sighed. D.J. was right. Danny Tanner, Stephanie's dad, was host of *Wake Up, San Francisco*, a morning show on public TV. Her aunt Becky was Danny's cohost on the show. Stephanie was working there part-time, doing odd jobs. But it was too hard to keep up with school and friends and work, so she had finally quit.

"I do miss the extra money," Stephanie said. "But let's not talk about that. Let's come up with an idea for your project."

After a minute, Stephanie snapped her fingers. "I've got it!" she cried suddenly. "Remember that story Dad did on his TV show about the California economy? When he went to Sacramento to meet the governor?"

D.J. let out a laugh. "You mean when he tried

to vacuum the governor's mansion? I remember that the governor threw him out."

Stephanie laughed too. "And they made him promise not to come back!" Their father was a total neat freak. He was always cleaning! It was a family joke.

Stephanie stopped laughing when their uncle Jesse entered the kitchen. He wore a very grim expression.

"What's wrong, Uncle Jesse?" she asked.

"I'm in a real bind," he told her.

Buzzzzz! The oven timer rang.

"Cookies!" Nicky and Alex yelled out happily. "Cousin Stephanie! The cookies are ready!"

"Uh, just a second, Uncle Jesse," Stephanie said.

She grabbed an oven mitt and pulled the cookie sheet from the oven. Mmmm! The cookies were perfect. Nicky and Alex looked on hungrily as Stephanie slid them onto a plate to cool.

"So, you were saying?" Stephanie asked when she was done.

"I need someone to fill in for me tomorrow night," Jesse said. "It's my turn to make dinner for the family, but I have to go out. I wouldn't ask if it weren't an emergency."

"What's the emergency?" D.J. asked.

"My anniversary," Jesse answered. "I'm getting

concert tickets. Becky's been dying to see Jimmy Lee Jasper, and tickets go on sale Wednesday. I have to wait on line tomorrow night to get a number to line up to buy tickets Wednesday morning."

"Wow, Jimmy Lee Jasper! Becky's gonna flip!" Stephanie exclaimed.

Jesse beamed. "She sure is! Becky loves country music. So anyway, can you two help me out?"

D.J. pushed away from the table and scooped up her backpack. "Sorry, Uncle Jesse. I'd love to help you, but I can't. I'll be in the library all day tomorrow and tomorrow night too. In fact," D.J. joked, "you might as well send my meals there for the next few days." She sighed. "I'll be there every waking minute."

D.J. slung her backpack over her shoulder and headed for the stairs.

"Well, I can help you, Uncle Jesse," Stephanie said. "I'll be glad to make dinner tomorrow night."

Jesse eyed her uncertainly. "I don't know, Steph," he said. "I was thinking maybe you and D.J. could do it together. But—"

"I can do it myself!" Stephanie insisted. "Really!"

"Have you ever cooked before?" Jesse asked.

"Who, me? Of course I have!" Stephanie held up the plate of cookies. "See? I made these cookies all by myself." She handed one to Nicky and one to Alex.

"Yummy!" they raved in between bites. "Cousin Stephanie is a good cook, Daddy!"

Jesse shook his head. "That's not cooking, Stephanie. That's just opening a tube of dough and putting it on a cookie sheet. This means making supper for nine people," Jesse reminded her.

Stephanie took a bite of a cookie herself and thought for a moment. "Well, I make my lunch for school all the time," she said. "Dinner is just like lunch, except it's hot."

Jesse stared at her for another minute. "Well, okay," he finally said. "If you think you can."

"Excellent!" Stephanie clasped her hands together excitedly. "Now, let's see . . . what should I make? How about a big, juicy pot roast? Or a turkey with all the trimmings?"

"Whoa! Hold on a second!" Jesse interrupted. "Just make some pasta and open a jar of sauce."

Stephanie nodded. "Right. Pasta. Sauce. Something totally simple." She smiled and handed him a freshly baked cookie. "Don't worry about a thing. Chef Stephanie has dinner under control!"

CHAPTER
2

♦ ◂ ◗ ♦

Stephanie rushed home the next day after school. She still had a few hours before she needed to start dinner. Luckily, she'd finished all her homework in study hall that afternoon. She could relax for a while and then think about cooking.

The living room was empty. *Excellent!* she thought. She turned on the television and flipped through the channels.

Nothing! The whole TV to myself and there's nothing on!

Just then a title flashed across the screen. *Cooking with Chef Thelma.*

"Hey!" Stephanie exclaimed. "This might come in handy." She found a pen and a pad of paper and sat down on the sofa.

Chef Thelma appeared, smiling. "Welcome, viewers! Today I will show you how to make an incredible dinner. It is so delicious, your family will beg for more!" she promised. "Now, first off, you'll need these ingredients . . ."

Stephanie scribbled furiously as Chef Thelma called off the ingredients for the recipes. "Lamb chops, olive oil, tarragon . . ."

Stephanie wrote as fast as she could, but it was tough writing and watching TV at the same time. Tarragon? she wondered. Was that a vegetable? A kind of noodle? She'd never heard of it before. She wondered if she could find it in the supermarket.

By the time the show was over, Stephanie had recipes for an incredible dinner. "Breaded chicken fingers, broiled lamb chops, and gourmet tricolor salad," she read from her notes. "This will be the best dinner the Tanners ever tasted!"

The front door swung open. "Hey, Steph," Danny called as he hung his jacket on a hook by the door.

"Hi, Dad!" Stephanie replied. "Can you take me to the store right away?"

Danny looked at the jacket that he'd just hung up. "Uh, do you have to go right now?" he asked.

"Yes. I'm cooking dinner tonight and I need groceries."

"You're cooking dinner?" Danny asked.

"Yup. I'm filling in for Uncle Jesse," Stephanie explained. "He said it was a life-or-death thing, so I'm helping him out."

Danny removed his jacket from the hook. "Okay, honey," he said with a yawn. "Let's go."

Stephanie folded the recipes and stuffed them in her pocket. Boy, was everyone going to be surprised. This was going to be the dinner to end all dinners! Chef Thelma had promised.

An hour later Stephanie flew into the kitchen and set her grocery bags down on the table. Her nine-year-old sister, Michelle, glanced up from her homework.

"What's in the bags?" Michelle asked.

"Stuff for dinner," Stephanie replied. She began unpacking the groceries.

Michelle lifted a package stuffed with green leaves. She wrinkled her nose in distaste. "What's this?"

Stephanie took the bag. "It's arugula. It's for the tricolor salad," she explained. "It's a salad made with three colors of lettuce."

"I thought all lettuce was green," Michelle said.

"Listen, Michelle," Stephanie said, "I don't have time to teach you about lettuce now, I need to start

11

dinner. So, please . . . pretty please . . . get out of the kitchen?"

Michelle's eyes widened. "You're making dinner tonight? Do you know how?"

Stephanie's smile faded. "Of course I do! Now, please . . . do your homework somewhere else."

Michelle shrugged. "What time will dinner be ready?"

Stephanie glanced at the clock. It was four-thirty. "At the usual time. Six-thirty," she said.

For the next two hours Stephanie mixed and stirred, baked and broiled. The aroma in the kitchen was incredible! Cooking was fun!

At six-thirty Danny struck his head into the kitchen. "Steph? How's it going?"

Stephanie lit the tall dinner candles she had placed on the table. "Everything's ready, Dad," she said. "Call in the troops!"

Danny stared at the dinner table. "Wow," he said. He leaned through the door and called in the family.

Jesse was the first to step into the kitchen. "Hey, thanks, Steph," he whispered. "I got the tickets and—" He stopped in surprise. His mouth fell open. "What's all this?"

Stephanie stood proudly next to the table. It was set with the family's best china and white linen dinner napkins. She had filled bread baskets with steaming hot biscuits. She even put out separate salad forks for her tricolor salad.

"This looks like a banquet," Jesse said. "Not a Tuesday-night family dinner! What's going on?"

Becky stepped into the kitchen. She stared at the table too. "Steph, this is amazing!" she said.

Joey Gladstone was the next to arrive. Joey was Danny's best friend from college. He lived with Stephanie's family too.

Joey was a comedian. He cohosted a radio show with her uncle Jesse. The show was called *The Rush Hour Renegades.* Joey told jokes and did impressions.

Joey always had something funny to say. But tonight he was practically speechless. He gaped at the dinner table. "Steph," Joey said, "you really did all this?"

"I sure did," Stephanie said.

"It smells fantastic in here!" D.J. hurried in with her backpack. "I was going to head back to the library, but now I think I'll stay for dinner!"

Stephanie pointed to the name cards next to all the plates. "I made name cards," she said. "So everyone knows where to sit."

"But we always sit in the same place," Michelle reminded her.

"I know," Stephanie said. "But Chef Thelma said this is what fancy people do for dinner parties." She cleared her throat. "Please, everyone," she said very formally, "won't you sit down? Dinner is served."

Everyone sat. Joey reached for the bread basket. "Homemade biscuits!" he exclaimed. "And they're still hot!"

Stephanie served the salad on small plates. Becky took one bite and nodded with approval.

"Stephanie! This is delicious!" she exclaimed. "What kind of salad is this?"

"Try-to-color salad," Michelle replied. "With a rutabaga."

Everyone stared at her. Stephanie giggled. "She means tricolor salad with arugula."

Stephanie served the chicken fingers. "There's honey-mustard sauce to go with them," she said. "And that's just the appetizer!"

Danny took a bit of chicken. "Sweetie, I'm impressed! This is very good!"

"Thanks, Dad."

In a few minutes Stephanie brought out the main course. She placed a perfectly broiled lamb chop on each plate. Then she dished out nine helpings of vegetables.

"Boy, you really went all out," Joey remarked.

"Stephanie," Jesse said, "I admit that I was worried about this dinner. But this is all delicious!"

"Thanks, Uncle Jess." Stephanie beamed.

Becky suddenly put down her fork. "Wait a minute!" she said. "Jesse, wasn't it your turn to cook dinner tonight?"

Jesse stopped chewing. He cast a nervous glance at Stephanie.

"Uh, yes, Aunt Becky," Stephanie said quickly. "But I begged him to let me cook instead. Because I . . . I'm planning to cook a big dinner for some friends and I needed the practice!"

Becky continued to eat. "Well, I wouldn't worry about practicing," she said. "You really have a talent for cooking!"

Stephanie's smile grew even wider. She could hardly believe it. The whole family was raving about her first real meal!

"You know," Joey said through a mouthful of vegetables, "this is just as good as the food I had the other night. At that fund-raiser dinner for the radio station. And it was catered by one of the fanciest chefs in San Francisco. He charged a fortune for it too."

"Thanks, Joey," Stephanie replied. "I mean, I always liked cooking, but now I feel so . . . so—"

Wait a minute!

"Joey!" Stephanie cried. "You've just given me the most amazing idea!"

Joey stopped gnawing on his lamb chop bone. "Hmmm?" he asked.

"A catering business—cooking for people and getting paid! I could do that! I could start my own catering business!"

And make enough money to buy a great gift for Uncle Jesse and Aunt Becky, she added to herself. She cast an excited glance at D.J.

"But, Stephanie," D.J. interrupted, "you don't know the first thing about starting a business. It takes research and—"

"Oh, D.J.! I'm a fabulous cook! Everyone says so. Can I do it, Dad?" Stephanie asked.

Danny shrugged. "I don't see why not," he said. "But D.J. is right. First you need to go to the library and take out some books on how to start a business. Then you can write to the . . ."

Stephanie was only half listening to her father. She was already trying to come up with a name for her new catering business. Stephanie's Super Suppers? Gourmet Goodies to Go?

"Hold on, Stephanie!" D.J. cried. "I just got an even better idea!"

Stephanie looked up. "You did?"

D.J. nodded. "Yes! It's the perfect topic for my economics presentation!"

Stephanie seemed confused. "What is?"

"How to run a successful business!" D.J. exclaimed. "You start a catering business, and I'll record the whole thing for my presentation!"

"You mean I'm going to be the subject of your big economics project?" Stephanie beamed. "All right!" She slapped a high-five with her sister.

"D.J.," Stephanie announced, "this is one project where I can positively, definitely promise you an A plus!"

CHAPTER
3

◆ ◢ ◢ ◆

"If you're such a great cook, then why are you buying your lunch today?" Stephanie's best friend, Darcy Powell, grinned at Stephanie. They were waiting on line at the school cafeteria.

Stephanie had just finished telling Darcy about the excellent dinner she'd made the night before.

"I'm buying my lunch because I didn't have time to make anything this morning," she explained. "And anyway, I like the school pizza."

Darcy shook her head, making her dark curls bounce. "You like cafeteria food?" She chuckled.

"Just the pizza," Stephanie replied. "And the fried chicken."

Darcy made a gagging noise and Stephanie

laughed. Darcy always made her laugh—ever since they'd become friends two years earlier, when Darcy moved to San Francisco from Chicago.

"Don't joke," Allie Taylor stated. Allie was Stephanie's other best friend. She and Allie were so close, they were practically sisters. They'd been friends ever since kindergarten, when their teacher sat them next to each other.

Allie had wavy brown hair and soft green eyes. She could be quiet—especially around boys—but she was lots of fun. "I think it's great," Allie added.

"You think cafeteria food is great too?" Darcy asked Allie in disgust.

"No," Allie said. "I think it's great that Stephanie can cook! You know I love cooking. The first meal I learned to make was scrambled eggs and cinnamon toast. I learned when I was seven and—"

Stephanie and Darcy groaned. Sometimes when Allie started telling stories, she didn't know when to stop.

"We've heard the cinnamon toast story before," Stephanie reminded her. She slid her tray toward the cash register and paid. She waited for Darcy and Allie. Then they all carried their lunches to their usual table.

She, Allie, and Darcy had lunch period together.

For two years now they'd made it a habit of sitting at the third table from the back of the cafeteria.

"Anyway, I haven't told you guys the best part of *my* story yet," Stephanie added as they sat down.

"What's that?" Allie asked.

"I'm starting my own catering business!" Stephanie announced.

Darcy and Allie looked at each other across the table. "A cooking business? You?" Allie asked.

"Sure. Everyone loved the dinner I made last night. So I realized I could cook for other people— and earn money," Stephanie explained. "I'll make a fortune!"

Allie began to eat her pizza. "Stephanie," she said in between bites, "are you sure you can handle a real business?"

Stephanie shrugged. "Why not? Joey said my dinner was better than one he had last week. And that was at a fund-raiser for the radio station. And it was catered by a famous chef!"

Allie eyed her suspiciously. "Joey really said your cooking was better than a famous chef's?"

"He said it was just as good," Stephanie replied.

"And nobody was rushed to the hospital with food poisoning or anything?" Darcy joked.

Stephanie made a face. "Very funny, Darcy. You know, Allie's not the only good cook around here."

Allie and Darcy giggled.

"You don't believe me, do you?" Stephanie said.

"It's not that, Steph," Allie told her. "I mean, I'm sure the dinner you cooked was good, but sometimes you kind of . . ."

"What?" Stephanie demanded.

"Exaggerate a bit," Darcy finished.

"Well, I'm not exaggerating this time!" Stephanie told them.

"Really, Stephanie," Allie said in a gentle tone. "I'm glad you had fun cooking. But really good cooking is a talent, like being an artist or something. And—"

"And you don't think I have any talent!" Stephanie folded her arms across her chest.

"I didn't say that," Allie defended herself. "But cooking one good meal doesn't make you a chef. Now, I've been cooking since—"

"Since you were seven, I know, I know," Stephanie grumbled. "Just because I started only yesterday doesn't mean I'm not as good a cook as you."

"No offense, Steph. But you really couldn't be as good as me," Allie said.

"Why not?" Stephanie felt annoyed. "Listen,

Allie, I'll prove what a good cook I am," she insisted.

"How are you going to do that?" Allie asked.

"Simple," Stephanie answered. "I'll make a special dinner—just for you guys. How about next Sunday? Bring your parents. Your whole families! I'll make us a banquet!"

Allie stared at her in disbelief. "Stephanie, that's an awful lot of work!" she said.

"Oh, please!" Stephanie shrugged. "It's nothing for me."

"Ugh. I can't even think about cooking," Darcy said. "You know, I tried to make spaghetti for my family once, but I boiled it too long. The noodles fell apart and it looked like oatmeal. Then there was another time when I—"

"I think the big dinner is a great idea," Stephanie interrupted. "I'll have fun doing it. I'll watch all the cooking shows I can this week. You'll see."

"I don't know," Allie said. Suddenly her eyes lit up. "Hey! Why don't we cook the meal together? I could bring over some of my special recipes. Now, that would be major fun!"

"Cool," Darcy said with a grin. "I won't mind cooking if we all do it. And I'll just bring my parents, since my big sister is away at college, and—"

Stephanie held up her hand. "Whoa! Hold on a

sec, you guys! I don't think cooking together is going to work."

"Why not?" Allie asked.

Because it was my idea, Stephanie thought.

"Well, because," she said out loud. "I'd just rather cook alone."

Allie looked hurt. "You mean you don't want me to help at all?"

"Well, I don't want to hurt your feelings, but the whole point is to prove that I can cook. Besides—" She hesitated.

"Besides what?" Darcy asked.

"If you guys try to help, you might get in the way. You know that old saying, 'Too many cooks . . . uh . . . are spoiled by . . . no, they spoil the . . .' " Stephanie frowned. "I don't remember the exact saying. But it means you need one person in charge in the kitchen. Not three."

"Well, if you really think you can do it yourself, okay," Allie said. "But your whole family, me and my parents, and Darcy and her parents are a lot of people to cook for. Believe me, I know."

"Like I *don't* know?" Stephanie rolled her eyes. "Please. I just cooked a three-course dinner for nine!" she said. "How much trouble could it be to cook for only six more?"

CHAPTER
4

◆ ◀ ▪ ◆

After school Stephanie sat at her uncle Jesse's computer. She was trying to come up with a flier design. She wanted to advertise her catering business around the neighborhood. If she was going to earn enough to buy Uncle Jesse and Aunt Becky a really great anniversary present, she needed some jobs lined up fast.

She stared at the blank computer screen for fifteen minutes. She couldn't even come up with a business name!

The name should say something about great food, she thought. She typed GREAT FOOD. *No. Too plain.*

Maybe I should play up the biscuits, she thought. *Everyone raved about them.*

She typed BISCUITS 'R' US. But that sounded as if she knew how to make only biscuits.

Stephanie stared at the blank screen a little while longer. It was probably a good idea to use her name in the title. Like Mrs. Fields's cookies, and Paul Newman's salad dressing.

TANNER'S, she typed. "Tanner's what?"

What had Joey said about her food? That it was tasty?

"I've got it!" she cried. "Tanner's Tasties!"

TANNER'S TASTIES

We Cater All Parties—All Sizes
Homemade Biscuits Are Our Specialty!
Ask about our delicious lamb chops!

She added her phone number and printed out fifty copies. When the fliers were ready, she pulled on her denim jacket, grabbed a roll of masking tape, and ran outside.

Stephanie taped a flier to every lamppost on her block. Then she tucked one under the windshield of every parked car. She was a few doors away from her house when her father's car turned up the street.

"Hi, Stephanie," Danny called through the open window. "What are you doing?"

"Hi, Dad. I'm advertising for my new catering business."

Danny narrowed his eyes. "Already?" he asked. "I thought you were going to do some research on starting a business first. There are tons of books in the library about that subject."

Stephanie shrugged. "What's there to research?" she asked. "I just have to advertise, take orders, and cook."

Danny reached for a flier. "It says here, 'We cater all parties,' " Danny pointed out. "Who is 'We'?"

"I'm 'We'!" Stephanie replied.

"Isn't anyone helping you?" Danny asked.

Stephanie shook her head. "Nah, I don't need any help."

Danny looked doubtful. "Stephanie, running a business is a lot harder than you think. Maybe D.J. can help you. Or Allie and Darcy. Did you ask them?"

Stephanie placed a flier on her father's windshield. "Don't worry, Dad," she said matter-of-factly. "I have everything under control. So, are you going to be my first customer?"

Danny thought for a moment. "Well, you know, I could use a cake. Kelly Fishman from our office just got engaged. I need to give her some kind of a gift. A cake would be perfect. How much would a cake cost?"

Stephanie frowned. She hadn't given stuff like prices much thought yet. "How about ten dollars?" she asked.

"Sounds fair." Danny reached for his wallet. He took out a five-dollar bill and handed it to Stephanie.

"Here's half the money," he said. "I'll pay you the rest when the cake is done. Could you have it on Friday morning? I could give Kelly the cake then, so she'll have it for the weekend. Her fiancé is coming to town on Sunday. Oh, and could you write a message on the cake?" Danny added.

"Sure, I can do that," Stephanie answered. She clutched the money in her hand. Her first sale! This was so exciting!

"Write 'Congratulations on Your Engagement,' " Danny said.

Stephanie reached into her backpack. She whipped out a small pad and a pen. She scribbled down the order. She had barely finished writing, when she heard someone calling her name from across the street.

"It's Mrs. Lodge," Stephanie said to her dad. "I'll see you at home in a little while."

As her father pulled away, Stephanie dashed across the street to the Lodges' house.

"Hi, Mrs. Lodge!" she called out.

"Hello, Stephanie. How are you?" Mrs. Lodge tried to smooth down her rumpled hair. She had four kids, all younger than Michelle, who was nine. Plus she had two dogs and two cats. She always looked totally frazzled.

"I'm okay," Stephanie told her.

Mrs. Lodge held up Stephanie's flier. "Is this you, by any chance?" she asked. "Tanner's Tasties?"

Stephanie smiled proudly. "Yes, that's me!" she said.

"Great!" Mrs. Lodge said. "You are the answer to my prayers! Amy's fifth birthday is next Sunday. The place where I was going to have her party just closed. By now every other place is booked. I have to have the party here at the house, and there's no time to plan the menu. Can you cater it?"

Stephanie's eyes lit up. "Oh, yes! Definitely!"

Mrs. Lodge let out a relieved sigh. "Fantastic."

Stephanie lifted her pad and pen again. "How many kids will there be?" she asked.

"Ten five-year-olds."

"And what kind of food do you want?" Stephanie asked. "Lamb chops? Tricolor salad?"

28

Mrs. Lodge laughed. "That sounds a bit sophisticated for five-year-olds. How about baked ziti? It's Amy's favorite."

"Baked ziti?" Stephanie wasn't exactly sure how to make baked ziti, but she didn't want Mrs. Lodge to know that. "That's just pasta, cheese, and sauce, right?"

"Right," Mrs. Lodge answered.

"Then of course I can make baked ziti!" Stephanie said. "I'll make you the best baked ziti in San Francisco!"

"Oh—and I'll need a birthday cake," Mrs. Lodge said. "Anything but chocolate. Amy is allergic to chocolate."

"One birthday cake. Not chocolate," Stephanie repeated. She jotted down the order on her pad. "No problem, Mrs. Lodge. But I'll need half the money today. To buy the ingredients and stuff."

Mrs. Lodge reached into her purse. "Here's twenty-five dollars," she said, handing the money to Stephanie. "Is that enough?"

Stephanie's eyes brightened at the sight of the crisp new bills. "Perfect!" she cried. "See you next Sunday!"

As she ran back to her house, Stephanie clutched her money tightly inside her denim jacket pocket. In a few minutes she already had two orders—and made thirty dollars! This catering business was awesome!

Stephanie flew up the driveway and reached for the front doorknob. Before she could open the door, out walked Joey and Michelle. They were on their way to Michelle's softball game. Joey was their coach. They had practice one or two times a week and a game every Sunday.

"Hey, guys! Guess what?" Stephanie said excitedly. "I already have two orders for my new catering business!"

"Excellent!" Joey said. "How about a third?"

Stephanie's mouth fell open. "Seriously?"

Joey nodded. "Yup. I was thinking of buying a cake for my friend Samantha," he explained. "She's having major boyfriend problems, and I thought it might cheer her up. But then I thought, Why buy a cake when the best cook in town lives right under my roof?"

Stephanie giggled. "Thanks, Joey!" She took out her pad again. "That's one more cake."

Joey leaned over. "Uh, Steph, could you write 'Dump the Jerk' on the cake?" he asked.

Stephanie laughed. "Sure. Consider it done."

Joey smiled. "Great. I'll leave it on her doorstep next weekend, before she goes on vacation. How much?"

"Ten dollars," Stephanie replied. "But I'll need half up front."

Joey took five crumpled singles from his pocket and handed them to Stephanie.

"Can I order something too?" Michelle asked.

Stephanie stared at her little sister. "Michelle, you don't have any money."

"I know, but our softball team is having a bake sale next Sunday. I could sell brownies or cookies for you—if you give half of the money you make to the team."

Stephanie thought it over for a second. This was a great chance to make some new customers! "Michelle, that's an excellent idea! Consider it done. How about four dozen brownies?" She wrote it on her list. "For next Sunday."

Stephanie hurried up the steps to D.J.'s room and knocked on her sister's door.

"Come in!" D.J. called.

Stephanie flung open the door. She tossed the thirty-five dollars she had just collected carelessly in the air—just like she'd seen people in the movies do. The bills fluttered and landed on D.J.'s bed.

"What's that?" D.J. asked.

"I've gotten four orders already!" Stephanie exclaimed proudly.

"So fast?" D.J. asked. "Wow! Now that you're a

rich workingwoman, do you want to chip in with me for an anniversary present for Uncle Jesse and Aunt Becky? I was thinking of buying tickets for a show or something," D.J. said. "Dad and Joey said they'd chip in too."

"I don't think so," Stephanie said. "I kind of wanted to get them something on my own."

"Like what?" D.J. asked.

"Like a new Jimmy Lee Jasper CD?"

"Becky probably has them all," D.J. said. "And Jesse doesn't like Jimmy Lee much anyway. Besides, Jesse and Becky's CD player hasn't been working for weeks."

That's it! Stephanie thought. *They need a new CD player! Now, that's a present they'll never forget.*

"Uh, my present is a surprise," Stephanie told D.J. "A very big surprise!"

CHAPTER
5

◆ ◀ ◗ ◆

It was Monday afternoon. Stephanie had just raced home from school to get the TV to herself. She dropped her book bag on the floor by the door and tossed her jacket on a hook. And halted in shock. Michelle was already sitting on the sofa, watching TV.

Stephanie took a deep breath. "Michelle, can I ask you a really big favor?"

Michelle stared at the flickering screen. "Hmmm?"

"Can you watch TV upstairs in Aunt Becky's apartment? I need to watch a few shows on cable."

Michelle glanced up. "What shows?" she asked.

"*Cooking with Chef Thelma, Wong's Chinese Cook-*

ing, oh, and the All-Food Network," Stephanie replied.

Michelle looked surprised. "You're kidding."

Stephanie shook her head. "Nope. So, if you don't mind . . ." She picked up the remote and changed the channel.

"Hey!" Michelle cried. "I was here first." She grabbed back the remote.

It sure is hard to run a business with a little sister around, Stephanie thought. She would tell D.J. to mention that in her project.

"Here's the thing, Michelle," she said. "I've switched chores with everyone, and now I'm cooking dinner every night this week. Now—if I don't watch these cooking shows, I won't know what to cook. And if I don't know what to cook, you won't have anything good to eat!"

"Oh!" Michelle handed the remote control back to Stephanie. "That's different. Do you need any help?"

Stephanie rolled her eyes. "Thanks, Michelle. I would *love* you to help me, really. But I'm cooking dinner to practice for my catering business, and I really need to do it all myself."

Michelle nodded. "Okay," she said. "I'll leave you alone. I sure hope one of those shows tells you how to make a really fantastic pizza."

As soon as Michelle was gone, Stephanie sank down onto the couch. She picked up her pad and pencil just as Chef Thelma's show came on. Frantically, she scribbled ingredients as Chef Thelma called them out.

Today there were special international recipes. Hawaiian grilled salmon, Mexican chili pie, Spanish rice pilaf, and Japanese chicken teriyaki. Chef Thelma said they were all impressive, but simple to make.

After two more hours of shows, Stephanie looked over the notes she had written. She had over fifteen recipes. More than enough for dinner every night this week. Including a great recipe for tangy meat loaf. That would be perfect for the big dinner with Allie's and Darcy's families.

The front door swung open and D.J. dragged herself in from another studying marathon in the college library.

Stephanie hopped off the sofa. "Deej! You have to take me to the store!"

D.J. sighed. "The store? Right now?" she asked wearily.

Stephanie nodded. "Yup. I have to get lots of new ingredients."

D.J. didn't move.

"Come on!" Stephanie insisted. "It's for the project, remember? If I can't cook, then my business will fail . . . and so will your project!"

D.J. grumbled, then opened her book bag. "I know, I know," she said. "Let me get my economics notebook. I need to take notes at the store." D.J. shook her head. "Just what I wanted to do—more work!"

Stephanie pulled D.J. into the kitchen with her. "I just need to grab some grocery money," Stephanie said.

She picked up the special canister that held the family grocery money. The grown-ups usually took turns doing the grocery shopping. They kept some money on hand for whoever needed to go to the store.

"Yikes. There's two fifty-dollar bills here," Stephanie said. "I was going to bring only twenty dollars or so."

"You might need more than twenty," D.J. told her. "Groceries are more expensive than you think. Take both bills."

"Really? Well, okay." Stephanie tucked the money carefully into her wallet. "I guess I don't have to spend all this, right?"

"Right," D.J. answered. "I don't think you need to spend one hundred dollars!"

Twenty minutes later they were roaming the aisles of the nearest supermarket.

"Look, D.J., gourmet walnuts!" Stephanie waved the bag over her head. "They're already shelled and chopped. They'll be perfect for my brownies for the softball team's bake sale."

D.J. took the bag from Stephanie's hands. "But these are so expensive," she pointed out. She held up another bag. "See here, this bag of walnuts is half the price. You should be trying to save money!"

"But those nuts are still in their shells," Stephanie said. "Think of all the time I'll save if I buy this bag." She tossed the expensive bag into her cart.

"Okay, but I think you're crazy," D.J. said. She wrote down the price of the nuts under "catering business."

They moved on to the next aisle.

"Tomato sauce next," Stephanie said, reading her shopping list. She stared blankly. There were rows and rows of cans and jars.

"I never knew there were so many brands of sauce to choose from!"

"Which do you need?" D.J. asked. "Sauce with meat, sauce with cheese, sauce with onions and peppers, or sauce with mushrooms?"

"I don't know. Which sauce goes best with baked ziti?" Stephanie asked.

"Don't ask me," D.J. told her.

"I know," Stephanie decided. "I'll just buy the ingredients and make the sauce myself. It will taste better if it's homemade."

"Do you know how to make tomato sauce?" D.J. asked. She held up a jar of tomato sauce. "Maybe you should just pick one of these. It will save time and money. You've never made tomato sauce before. How do you know what goes in it?"

Stephanie turned toward the vegetable aisle. D.J. followed. Stephanie counted out ten ripe tomatoes and flung them into her cart.

"Come on, Deej, how hard could it be to make tomato sauce? Think about it. What's in it? Tomatoes!"

D.J. handed her the jar of sauce. "Read the label," she said. "This sauce has water, oil, oregano, and basil."

Stephanie glanced at the bottom of the label and frowned as she kept reading. "And monosodium glutamate, calcium chloride, citric acid . . . yuck! I'm not putting any of that stuff in my sauce!"

"Stephanie, I really think it would be better and cheaper to buy the sauce. At least take one jar and try it," D.J. insisted.

"Okay, okay," Stephanie grumbled. She placed the jar in the shopping cart. "Maybe I'll use the jar of sauce for a family dinner."

"Then I'll write the price on the 'family grocery' list," D.J. told her.

Stephanie put her hands on her hips. "Listen, D.J., just let me handle the rest of the shopping, okay? I mean, who's the expert cook here anyway?"

"Shopping is one thing. This is also a lesson in keeping to a food budget," D.J. said. "And I don't think you're making the best economic choices."

"Don't worry," Stephanie assured her. "I have more than enough money with me, right? Thirty-five dollars for the catering groceries, and one hundred for the family meals. I'm spending only a tiny amount. And by this time next week, when all my customers have paid me, I'll have earned lots more for the business."

D.J. shook her head. "I still say you're spending way too much money today. You should be on a strict budget."

"Tell you what," Stephanie said. "I'll put back some of the things I need for the three cakes and the brownies. I won't make them till the end of the week anyway." Stephanie unloaded those items from her cart.

"See? I'm not spending too much," she told D.J. "Hey! Check this out, Deej!" She stopped pushing her cart and pulled a package off the shelf.

"They have that cool neon-colored cake icing!" Without checking the price, she tossed two tubes of the stuff into her cart.

"That will have to go under catering costs," D.J. said.

"D.J., you're driving me crazy. I'll figure the money out later, okay?" Stephanie said. "It's my responsibility."

D.J. shrugged. "Okay. If you're sure."

"I'm sure," Stephanie said. She finished the rest of the shopping and took her place on the check-out line.

"Hey! Look at these great aprons!" Stephanie grabbed an apron from a special display stand. The aprons all had bright lettering across the front. Stephanie chose one that said NOW I'M COOKIN!

"How can I *not* buy this, huh, Deej?" Stephanie tossed the apron into her shopping cart.

D.J. shook her head. "I have a bad feeling about this, Stephanie. You'd better check your budget."

"Would you stop worrying!" Stephanie said. "Tanner's Tasties is already a surefire success. Why don't you get the car and meet me out front?"

"All right," D.J. agreed. She left the store.

Stephanie moved up to the cash register. The clerk rang up the items in her cart.

"Seventy-three dollars!" Stephanie stared at the total in shock. That was more than she expected to pay. A *lot* more!

Stephanie paid and stuck the change and the receipt into the very bottom of her backpack. *I better not let D.J. see this receipt right now,* Stephanie thought. *I'll never hear the end of it.*

Stephanie would straighten out the budget later. *It can't be so bad,* she told herself. After all, most of what she bought was for the family's groceries. And even D.J. had said that it cost a lot to feed their family.

Still, Stephanie realized that she had no idea if she'd spent her whole thirty-five dollars or not.

Her stomach tightened. She swallowed hard.

Maybe D.J. was right. Maybe running a catering business wasn't as easy as it seemed!

CHAPTER
6

◆ ◀ ▪ ◆

As soon as they got home, Stephanie unloaded the groceries in the kitchen. The door swung open and Jesse stepped inside.

"Shhhh!" Jesse peered around the kitchen. "I don't want Becky to know I'm down here."

"Why not?" Stephanie whispered back.

Jesse took a step closer to Stephanie. He whispered again. "I have to make a phone call about the rest of my big anniversary surprise. Watch the door, would you, Steph?"

"All clear," Stephanie told him.

Jesse picked up the phone and began to dial.

"Hello, is this Fujimoto Restaurant?" he whispered into the phone. He waited a few seconds, then spoke again, this time a tiny bit louder.

"Uh, is this Fujimoto's? It is? Great!" He winked at Stephanie. "I'd like your best table for this Sunday night, please. For two."

Stephanie wondered what all the secrecy was about.

"What's that?" Jesse asked in alarm. "You're booked? But we're just a party of two! Can't you fit us at a small table in the very back? Or maybe we won't even need a table . . . we can eat standing up. Please? It's our anniversary and—"

Jesse grumbled, then slammed down the phone receiver. "I can't believe this!" he moaned. "They're booked solid! Do you know what that means?"

"That they don't have any tables?" Stephanie asked, trying to make a joke.

Jesse glared at her. "It means Becky is going to kill me! I promised her I'd make these reservations weeks ago. I meant to do it then, but when I called the first time, their line was busy. Then I forgot about it. Now what am I going to do?"

Stephanie walked over to her uncle and put her hand on his shoulder. "I'm sorry, Uncle Jesse. Isn't there another restaurant you can call?"

Jesse shook his head. "Becky has her heart set on Fujimoto's," he said.

Stephanie frowned. "Wait a minute! That's Japanese food, right? Like chicken teriyaki?"

Jesse stared at her. "Yeah. And it's a very expensive place." Jesse sat down at the kitchen table and put his head in his hands.

Stephanie reached into a drawer next to the oven. She pulled out her notes from the cooking show. A smile crept across her face.

"Uncle Jesse, I think I have the answer to your problem!" she said happily.

Jesse looked up.

"Why go out and spend all that money when I can cook you a delicious and romantic Japanese dinner—right here at home."

"You know how to make Japanese food?" Jesse asked.

"Sure! I have a terrific recipe," she said, showing him her notes. "Look—Chicken Teriyaki Supreme! Or I could take out a Japanese cookbook from the library to get another one if you like. I'll be cooking all day Sunday anyway—for Amy Lodge's birthday party, and for Allie's and Darcy's family dinner. It won't be a problem. Come on . . . it'll be my pleasure. Part of my anniversary gift to you and Becky!"

Jesse thought for a minute. "You are a good cook," he said, thinking out loud. "And Becky will certainly be surprised," he added. Jesse reached into his pocket and pulled out his wallet. "Here. I'll give you some money for the cost of the ingredients."

He pulled out twenty dollars. "This is all I have right now. Is it enough?" he asked.

Stephanie's eyes widened in delight. "More than enough," she answered. *I'm making more catering supply money already!* She gave a sigh of relief.

"Excellent!" she cried. "Then it's all settled! Mr. Katsopolis, you hereby have a reservation for two, for this Sunday night, at . . . Stephimoto's Restaurant! Happy anniversary!"

Jesse smiled. "Stephanie," he exclaimed, giving her a big hug, "you're a lifesaver!"

Stephanie grinned. Then she caught a glimpse of the clock on the kitchen wall. It was after five. Dinner was at six-thirty.

"Yikes!" she cried. "Uncle Jesse, I really have to get dinner started. It's getting late."

Jesse smiled and rubbed his hands together. "So what are we having tonight?" he asked.

"Chili pie and eggplant Parmesan!" Stephanie beamed.

"Together?" Jesse asked.

"Sure. Tonight is International Surprise Night!" she proclaimed. "I got all these great recipes from Chef Thelma's show. If they're good, I'm going to add them to my catering menu. I can cater International Surprise Nights all over San Francisco!"

Stephanie turned on the stove and began warming up the beans for the chili. She made the pie crust and set it aside. Then she sliced the eggplant and put it in a deep baking dish. She hesitated. She needed to add tomato sauce.

Stephanie frowned. There was no time to make her own sauce tonight. She sighed and opened the jar of ready-made sauce that D.J. had made her buy.

I guess D.J. will say a big "I told you so" about this, she thought. *Oh, well.*

She added the sauce to the dish. Then she turned on the oven and slid it inside.

She was slicing cucumbers for a salad when Michelle, Nicky, and Alex walked through the kitchen on their way down to the basement. They each carried an armful of art supplies.

"Hey, guys," Stephanie said, "what's going on?"

"We're making a garage!" Nicky said proudly.

Michelle giggled. "Nicky, it's not a garage," she explained, "it's a collage. I'm helping the twins make a collage of different pictures of all of us. It's for Uncle Jesse and Aunt Becky," she told Stephanie. "For their anniversary gift."

"Oh," Stephanie said. "That's a nice idea." *But not quite a CD player!*

"Do you want to help?" Michelle asked.

"Nope. I'm cooking up my own present," Stephanie joked. "A special anniversary dinner. Plus, I'm buying them something they're going to love! Something *big.*"

"Wow," Michelle said. She turned to Nicky and Alex. "Come on, guys. Let's get this stuff downstairs."

When they were gone, Stephanie chopped a red pepper and began to think. She really had to get that CD player soon.

She'd get paid on Sunday. There was probably a way to pay the CD player off bit by bit. Say, ten dollars every week. The way her business was going, that would be no problem. So why not order it now?

Stephanie washed her hands and opened the kitchen drawer. She pulled out the phone book and found what she was looking for—Cooper Electronics. The family bought lots of their equipment from Mr. Cooper. She picked up the telephone and dialed the number.

"Hi, Mr. Cooper," Stephanie said. "This is Stephanie Tanner." She explained that she wanted to order a portable CD player and headphones. "I don't have all the money now," she added. "Could I pay a little bit each week?"

Mr. Cooper agreed that she could put down a fifty-dollar deposit and give him the rest in regular payments.

"No problem, Mr. Cooper. I'll bring the deposit over as soon as I have it," she promised.

Stephanie hung up the phone. It shouldn't take too long to earn the money. Why, by this weekend the CD player would practically be paid for!

Uncle Jesse and Aunt Becky were really going to be surprised. And it was all so simple.

As easy as . . . chili pie!

CHAPTER
7

♦ ◂ ◣ ♦

Brrriiing!

The phone rang as soon as Stephanie hung up. *That's weird,* she thought. *Is Cooper Electronics calling me back?*

But Allie's voice greeted her. "Hey, Steph," Allie said. "Darcy and I did all our homework in study hall today. So our parents said we can catch an early movie! We're going to see *The Big Break.* Want to come?"

"Do I!" Stephanie said. "I've been dying to see it for weeks! But I can't," she added. "Don't you remember? I have to cook dinner tonight."

"Oh. Sorry, I did forget," Allie said.

"Yeah, but I'm taking my cooking very seriously," Stephanie said.

"Sure I do. I just forgot temporarily," Allie told her.

"Well, I'm much too busy for movies. I happen to be in the middle of making a very special chili pie," Stephanie told her. "I'm just heating the lentil beans now."

"Lentil beans?" Allie shrieked. "Stephanie, that's the wrong beans. You need kidney beans. Or black beans or red beans, depending on what style you're making."

"Style of what?" Stephanie asked.

"Chili. Mexican style or California style," Allie told her.

"Uh, of course. I knew that!" Stephanie bluffed. "But, um, this is a new style. With lentils. It's, uh, Italian chili," she made up. "To go with eggplant Parmesan."

"Never heard of it," Allie said.

"Well, you don't know absolutely everything about cooking," Stephanie told her.

Joey stuck his head in the kitchen and waved, trying to catch Stephanie's attention. "Steph, how's dinner coming?" he called. "Is it almost ready? I'm starved."

"In a minute, Joey," she said. Joey nodded and disappeared. Stephanie spoke into the phone again. "Listen, Al, I've got to go. See you tomorrow at school." Stephanie hung up before Allie could answer.

Stephanie turned off the burner on the stove under the lentil beans. No wonder they didn't look quite right. Chef Thelma *had* said kidney beans. But Stephanie thought the lentil beans looked more interesting in the store. She didn't know you had to follow recipes so *exactly*.

She searched the cabinets. Finally, she found a bag of red kidney beans hiding behind the cereal.

"I guess I should have searched the cabinets before I went shopping," Stephanie muttered. She grabbed the beans and poured them into a pot. She scooped out some chili powder and added it to the beans. She turned on the burner again.

Becky crept into the kitchen. She quietly reached for a bag of nacho chips, but stopped when Stephanie saw her.

"I'm sorry, Stephanie!" Becky said. "But the twins are really hungry. Dinner tonight is late for them. I have to put something in their stomachs."

"Sure, fine," Stephanie said. "I'm sorry it's so late."

"Is anything wrong?" Becky asked.

"Well, I kind of used the wrong beans," Stephanie admitted. "I have to start the chili over."

Becky groaned.

"Not to worry," Stephanie told her. "They're cooking now."

Becky peeked at the pot on the stove. "Uh, Steph," Becky said. "I hate to tell you this. But dried beans have to cook at least an extra hour if you didn't soak them in water first."

Stephanie stared at her in disbelief. "But—dinner is already late," she said.

"Sorry," Becky told her.

"Becky, take the nacho chips," Stephanie said. "And stall everyone! I'm cooking as fast as I can!"

Two hours later Danny popped his head into the kitchen. "Uh, Steph, sweetie," he said gently. "It's almost nine o'clock. And, well, we're all really, really hungry."

Stephanie groaned. "I know what time it is, Dad! And dinner is served," she said. "For better or worse," she added under her breath.

The family marched in. They stared grumpily at the dinner table.

"Smile, Steph," D.J. told her. She pointed a video camera at her.

"D.J.! Why are you taping this?" Stephanie asked. "This isn't a paying job. This is only practice cooking!"

"I told you," D.J. replied. "I have to record everything."

"Well, okay," Stephanie said. "Everybody, take your places, please." She took the eggplant from the oven, where it had been baking. She set it on a special serving platter on the table.

"Finally," Michelle grumbled. "I'm starving!"

Stephanie placed the chili pie next to the salad. She dropped into her seat, exhausted.

"Dig in, everyone," she said. "You'll forget how long you had to wait when you taste everything."

"Yuck! What's that?" Alex asked, peering at the beans and pie crust on his plate. "It looks like mud!"

"Shhhhh!" Jesse told him. "You'll upset Stephanie."

"I'll try the chili pie," Michelle said. "I love chili!"

Stephanie sat back in her chair and watched Michelle lift a spoonful to her mouth. Stephanie smiled hopefully.

Michelle's eyes began to tear and a strange look came over her face. She began to cough. Then choke.

Danny jumped up in alarm. "Michelle, what is it?" he asked.

Michelle couldn't answer. She leapt up and ran to the kitchen sink, knocking over her chair. She turned on the cold water and began gulping it straight from the faucet.

A second later Joey jumped out of his seat and ran to the sink, pushing Michelle out of the way.

"*Hot!*" he screeched before gulping cold water.

Seconds later Becky and Jesse lined up at the sink behind them. D.J. taped it all with her video camera.

Stephanie stared at them all in horror. "What is going on?" she cried.

"You've . . . burned us out!" Joey explained in between gulps of water.

Danny swallowed a whole glass of water in one gulp. He wiped his mouth, then turned to Stephanie. "Stephanie, how much chili powder did you put in the chili?" he asked.

"Uh, whatever the recipe called for," Stephanie replied nervously. "Four tablespoons, I think."

Danny's eyes widened. "Four *tablespoons*?" he cried. "Let me see that recipe!"

Stephanie found the recipe and gave it to her dad.

"Stephanie!" he cried. "The recipe calls for four *teaspoons!* Not four tablespoons! What were you thinking?"

"Oops," Stephanie gulped. "Sorry. I know I paid attention to the recipe. I mixed those beans right after—" She paused. "Right after Allie called!" She stared at her family. "It's Allie's fault," she cried. "Her phone call got me all mixed up!"

"Don't feel too bad," Danny told her.

"I don't," Stephanie told him. "I promise that this will never happen again. Because from now on, *no one* talks to me while I cook!"

"Well, nobody's at fault. It was an honest mistake," Danny told her.

"I guess. Uh, here," Stephanie said, lifting the platter of eggplant Parmesan. "Try this. It has *no* chili powder, I promise."

"Not me," Michelle said. "My tongue is still on fire from that chili!"

"Well, everyone else can try it," Stephanie told them.

"The eggplant does smell terrific!" Danny said.

"Then, eat up!" Stephanie dished a portion onto his plate.

Danny picked up his fork and took a bite. He smiled as he chewed. Then his smile began to fade.

Stephanie stared at him. "Well?" she asked. "Is it good?"

Danny smiled awkwardly. "Uh, it's . . . very unusual."

"Then you like it?" Stephanie asked him eagerly.

Danny swallowed with a large gulp. "There's

just one tiny little problem," he said. "Stephanie, this eggplant is still almost raw. Didn't you know that you're supposed to fry it before you bake it?"

Stephanie felt her cheeks flame in embarrassment. "You're supposed to fry it first?"

Michelle groaned. "You ruined something else?"

"Michelle," Becky scolded. "That's not nice to say."

The whole family exchanged looks of disappointment.

"Now what do we do?" Jesse asked. "Eat peanut butter sandwiches?"

"Not me," Joey exclaimed. "My mouth was set for eggplant Parmesan." He sprang up from the table and quickly dialed the phone. "Hello, Luigi's? I'd like an order delivered, please. Nine portions of eggplant Parmesan!"

Stephanie sunk down low in her chair. She couldn't believe it! She had ruined two dishes in one night!

"Well," she managed to say, "I was right about one thing. My International Surprise Night *was* a surprise—we couldn't eat a bite!"

CHAPTER
8

◆ ◀ ◆ ◆

"Hi, Stephanie!" Allie called cheerfully.

Stephanie looked up from her catering business notepad. It was the next morning, and Stephanie was waiting for Allie and Darcy at their usual morning meeting spot—the pay phone by the gym.

Allie and Darcy were both grinning. "What are you so happy about?" Stephanie asked them.

"We were just talking about the movie we saw last night," Allie said. "It was exciting. And so funny! Too bad you couldn't make it, Steph. You would have loved it."

"I know that," Stephanie grumbled. "And you know I was too busy to go."

Allie and Darcy exchanged glances. "Okay,

okay," Darcy said. "I didn't mean to make you cranky."

"I'm not cranky, I'm just tired. It's hard work, practicing for my catering business." Stephanie glanced down at her notepad again.

"What's that for?" Darcy asked, nodding toward the pad.

Stephanie sighed. "It's the budget for my business," she told them. "D.J. thinks I'm already in debt."

"Are you?" Allie asked.

"Not at all," Stephanie replied. Actually, she had been shocked to learn that she'd spent forty-eight dollars on the catering groceries and her new apron. That was thirteen dollars more than she started out with!

But then her uncle Jesse gave her twenty dollars. She wasn't in debt anymore. But she had only seven dollars left.

"I'm not worried," Stephanie bluffed. "After all, I'll be paid thirty-five dollars for the rest of my orders this weekend. And my uncle Jesse will give me more too. The only problem is the timing. I do need to buy ingredients for the birthday party on Sunday. And I need some money to send to Cooper Electronics. I'm buying a special gift for Uncle Jesse and Aunt Becky's anniversary."

"Can you borrow some money from you dad?" Allie asked. "I mean, you'll get paid on Sunday for everything, so you can pay him back then."

"Maybe," Stephanie said.

"What's the special gift?" Darcy asked.

"A CD player."

"A CD player!" Darcy shouted so loud, the whole hallway full of kids turned to stare. "Isn't that expensive?" she went on in a lower voice.

"A little," Stephanie admitted. "But Mr. Cooper agreed to let me pay it off, like, ten dollars a week toward the whole cost. So I should be able to afford it."

She yawned and covered her mouth. "Sorry," she said. "I was up late, figuring my budget and studying recipes last night. Catering is more work than I thought it would be."

"So I guess this isn't a good time to give you our lists, is it?" Darcy said.

"What lists?" Stephanie asked.

"You know, for the big dinner," Darcy reminded her. "Our families this Sunday? Their favorite dishes? Remember?"

Stephanie groaned. "I remember." She hesitated. "Listen, you guys," she said. "Maybe we could do the big dinner another night."

"Why?" Darcy teased. "Is the World's Greatest Chef having second thoughts?"

Stephanie gritted her teeth. "No, it's just that I'm kind of overbooked for Sunday."

"Well, let us help, Stephanie," Allie offered. "We'd like to! I can bring my favorite recipe folder. If it's too much work for you, just ask!"

"Sure," Darcy agreed. "Everyone doesn't have a talent for cooking. Or running a business. It's nothing to be ashamed of."

"I'm not ashamed!" Stephanie protested. "And I *do* have cooking talent. I cooked my entire family a fabulous meal, remember?"

Except for the disaster last night, she added silently. *But that wasn't my fault!*

"You don't have to cancel," Stephanie insisted. "And I don't need your help!"

"Okay, okay! Calm down," Darcy told her.

"Are you sure?" Allie asked.

"Absolutely," Stephanie replied. "So, show me the lists."

Allie took her list from her backpack. "Okay. My mother's favorite dish is stir-fried chicken over vermicelli. And my father's—"

"Vermicelli?" Stephanie asked. "What's that?"

"It's a kind of pasta."

"Can you buy it at the supermarket?" Stephanie wanted to know.

Allie shrugged. "I guess so. And my father's favorite dish is Texas chili."

"Great," Stephanie mumbled.

"Is that a problem?" Allie asked.

"Not anymore," Stephanie said. "I learned how to cook it perfectly last night." *Or how* not *to cook it,* she added to herself.

Stephanie turned to Darcy. "What about your parents?"

Darcy pulled a folded sheet of paper from her pocket. "Okay. My mother's favorite food is vegetarian lasagna. And my father's favorite dish is ratatouille," she said.

"Rata-what?" Stephanie asked.

"Ratatouille," Darcy repeated. "It's some kind of stewed vegetables thing."

"What if I just make a nice, big meat loaf for everyone?" Stephanie suggested.

Darcy shook her head. "My parents don't eat meat."

Stephanie sighed. So much for that idea. "Fine. Give me your lists, then."

The first bell rang. Stephanie shoved the papers into the pocket of her backpack.

"So, how about coming over to my house and

doing makeovers after school?" Darcy asked as they headed for class.

"Sounds like fun," Allie answered.

Stephanie shook her head. "Count me out, guys. After school I'm going straight to my room."

"For a punishment?" Darcy joked.

"No. To map out a schedule for all these cooking jobs," Stephanie replied. "Wish me luck!"

I'm going to need plenty of luck, Stephanie thought. It was after school. She sat at her desk and stared at her cooking schedule. It was impossible!

D.J. knocked at the door. "Steph, I have some questions for you," D.J. said, coming in. "For my econ project." D.J. peered closely at Stephanie. "You don't look so hot. Anything wrong?"

"Not really," Stephanie bluffed. "It's just that all my big jobs are on the same day. Sunday." She read the list out loud.

"First I have to make three cakes. One for Dad, one for Joey's friend, and one for Amy Lodge's birthday party," Stephanie said.

"Ouch. That is a problem," D.J. agreed. "But at least they're all the same thing," D.J. said.

"Hey! That's right!" Stephanie brightened. "That gives me an amazing idea. I'll just triple the recipe and make them all at once."

"Brilliant!" D.J. nodded in approval.

"Sure," Stephanie went on. "I'll bake them all on Thursday night. I'll give Dad's cake to him Friday morning, and keep the other two cakes in the fridge."

"That's a great way to save time." D.J. seemed impressed. "Not bad, Steph! And you were worried about your schedule!"

"Not really," Stephanie fibbed. She began scribbling happily in her notebook.

D.J. checked her own notes. "Now, how are your finances? Are you making any money yet? Maybe I should look over your notes," D.J. suggested.

"Uhh . . ." Stephanie quickly shut her notepad. "Money is such a tricky subject. I need some time to redo my records." She grabbed her notebook. "But look here—my schedule included the proper amount of cleanup time for each cooking project."

"Dad would be proud," D.J. admitted. "But let's get back to the budget."

"Oh, it's fine, I'm telling you," Stephanie replied casually. "Don't worry."

"But I am worried," D.J. said. "What if something goes wrong and you don't get paid? You never know what could happen. Your business might fail. And so will my project!"

"Tanner's Tasties is not going to fail!" Stephanie

insisted. "Stop worrying all the time, D.J." She reached under her bed and pulled out the Cooper Electronics catalogue.

"Here, look. This will show you how confident I am that Tanner's Tasties will be a big success," she said. "This is what I ordered for Uncle Jesse and Aunt Becky. For their anniversary." Stephanie pointed to the picture of the portable CD player.

D.J.'s eyes widened. "You ordered that?" she asked.

Stephanie nodded.

"But you can't possibly afford that!" D.J. exclaimed. "How are you ever going to pay for it?"

"D.J., you're forgetting one thing," Stephanie said calmly. "I'm a great cook. A great cook who is about to make a ton of money in the catering business. Why, soon I'll be able to buy everyone in the family their own portable CD player!"

D.J. was speechless.

"Really, Deej, I have three jobs lined up for one weekend. I can do anything," Stephanie insisted.

"Well, then, can you make something great for dinner tonight?"

"Tonight?" Stephanie blinked in surprise.

She'd forgotten all about cooking tonight's dinner!

"It's already after five-thirty," D.J. pointed out.

"Oh, great! It's almost time to eat," Stephanie said. "Now what am I going to do?"

CHAPTER
9

◆ ◀ ◗ ◆

"Uh, I guess everyone will want something delicious for dinner," Stephanie stalled. Her mind was racing. What was she going to cook?

"Yeah, we all love that meal we eat in the evening," D.J. told Stephanie. "And you're the one who makes it. You switched cooking chores with the rest of us for the whole week, remember?"

Stephanie dropped her head in her hands and groaned. "Would you believe I completely forgot?"

"Well, it's a good thing I reminded you," D.J. said. She glanced at the clock. "I'd love to help you, Steph, but I have too much work."

Stephanie frowned. "Join the club," she muttered. She left her chart and notebook in her room and ran down to the kitchen. She prayed there was something there to make for dinner.

She rummaged through the freezer. Nothing. Then she came across three packages of hot dogs.

"Hot dogs! Perfect!" she cried. Those were easy to make.

"Are you making dinner again, Stephanie?" Danny asked, walking into the kitchen. Stephanie thought he looked a little worried.

"Yes, Dad," she said. "But I'm keeping it simple tonight—hot dogs."

Danny seemed relieved. "Simple will be good."

Stephanie lined the hot dogs up on the broiler tray and stuck them in the oven. The phone rang. It was Allie.

"Hi, Steph," she said. "I'm over at Darcy's. You should see the wild hairdo we just gave her!"

Stephanie could hear Darcy cracking up in the background. "Great," she said.

"But that's not why we called," Allie went on. "We were just thinking—are you absolutely sure you don't need help making dinner on Sunday? You seemed awfully stressed all day at school."

"Well, actually . . ." For a second Stephanie considered taking her friends up on their offer. Having Darcy's and Allie's help sure would make life easier.

"I'd love to make my special duck in orange sauce," Allie offered. "Or even eggplant Parmesan. It's a family favorite."

"Naturally," Stephanie said.

"What's that supposed to mean?" Allie asked.

"Nothing. I just never realized you were such a food expert before," Stephanie said. "I mean, last night you knew all about kidney beans. And I suppose you're an expert eggplant fryer too."

"Well, I do have a special way to fry the eggplant so it isn't too oily," Allie admitted.

Stephanie groaned.

Darcy came on the line. "Hey, Steph—you should see what Allie did to my head! You'd die!" Darcy laughed hysterically.

Stephanie felt a pang of resentment. Sure, Darcy and Allie had plenty of time to have fun. They could fool around all they wanted. They didn't have a business to run!

"I'm sure it's a riot," she said stiffly.

"So, anyway, what about Sunday?" Darcy asked. "Allie's right. You seem totally stressed. Admit it— this catering stuff is too much for you. So, why not let us help?"

"For one thing, Darcy, you can't cook, remember?" Stephanie pointed out.

"I know. But Allie says she could teach even a total dummy to cook." Darcy giggled.

Stephanie made up her mind. No way was she going to have Allie and Darcy think that *she* was a total dummy!

"No thanks," she replied stubbornly. "I said I would do this on my own, and I will. Just be here at six on Sunday with your parents. And be ready to be blown away."

"If you're sure . . ." Darcy said.

"I am," Stephanie said into the phone. "And tonight's gourmet meal is calling me. I've got to go."

Stephanie hung up the phone before Darcy or Allie could say anything more.

She checked the hot dogs on the broiler. "Looking good," she murmured. She felt so relieved, she decided to set the table—Michelle's chore tonight. As she took out the plates, she suddenly realized she hadn't made anything to eat with the hot dogs. No side dishes!

Uh-oh. She checked the time. Almost six-thirty!

Stephanie flung open the refrigerator door and searched high and low. There must be something to go with the hot dogs.

No such luck. They were out of corn. And out of french fries. And there wasn't any cole slaw to be found. She searched the kitchen cabinets. *Nothing!*

She was just about to give up, when she spotted a bag of potatoes pushed into a corner. She grabbed a bunch, washed and peeled them, and stuck them in the microwave. They were soft in ten minutes. She quickly mashed them and added cream and butter.

"I should spice them up a little," she said to herself. She stared at the spices in the spice rack. She closed her eyes and pointed. "Eeny, meeny, miny, mo," she chanted. She opened her eyes.

"Paprika!" She flipped open the cover and sprinkled.

"Yikes! Is it supposed to be so red? Or did I just ruin the mashed potatoes?" she muttered.

She frantically stirred the potatoes until all the paprika was blended in. The kitchen door swung open. Her family trooped in.

"Hi, Steph. At it again?" Jesse asked nervously.

"Should I call Luigi's right now?" Joey joked.

"Let's wait until after we spit everything out," Michelle said.

Stephanie glared at her. "Ha-ha," she said. The oven timer went off. Stephanie fetched the hot dogs and carried them to the table. She set them next to the mashed potatoes.

"Looks good, Stephanie," Danny said. "But aren't you forgetting something?"

"No. Potatoes, hot dogs, mustard, salt, and pepper," she counted. "What's missing?"

Nicky and Alex called out the answer together. "Hot dog buns!"

Stephanie slapped her head. "Buns! I totally forgot! Hang on, I'll get some!" She ran to the freezer and opened the door. Not a bun in sight. "No buns," she said. "Sorry."

Everyone groaned. Then Joey interrupted with a loud "*Mmmmmmmm!*"

Everyone turned to stare.

"These potatoes are amazing!" he exclaimed. "Stephanie, these are the best mashed potatoes I've ever had in my life!"

Stephanie waited for him to finish the joke, but to her surprise, he kept on eating. "Really?" she asked.

Joey didn't answer. He was too busy stuffing his mouth with more potatoes. And so was everyone else.

"See?" she said happily. "I knew tonight's dinner wouldn't be a total disaster!"

"These *are* good," D.J. agreed. "If your budget is as good as this cooking, our project has nothing to worry about."

"Not a thing," Stephanie said.

She finished her meal in record time. Luckily, she didn't have dishwashing duty tonight! She stopped to get an extra drink of juice, then went to the bathroom. Finally, she raced to her room. She had to finish a new budget before D.J. saw the old one.

She pushed open her bedroom door—and saw D.J. standing at her desk.

"D.J.! How did you sneak in here? What are you doing?" she screeched. D.J. was already reading her catering notes.

"I need that," Stephanie cried, trying to pull the pad from D.J.'s hands.

"I can't believe this, Stephanie," D.J. said. "Do you know you have only seven dollars left in your entire budget?"

"Of course I know!" Stephanie replied casually. "Sure! Um, that was my plan."

"But, Stephanie, you have more groceries to buy. How could you spend so much, when you haven't been paid for a finished order yet?"

"Relax. I'll be paid soon," Stephanie pointed out. "In the meantime I can borrow from Dad. So, what's the problem? Really, D.J.," Stephanie said with a chuckle. "You're starting to sound like Dad. So fussy!"

"Stephanie, I'm not kidding," D.J. said. "You don't have enough money! Your business could fail! And so could my grade on this project!"

"D.J., you're forgetting one thing," Stephanie said calmly. "I'm a great cook. A great cook who is about to make a ton of money."

D.J. was speechless. "Stephanie, you're completely nuts," she said.

Stephanie grinned. "Maybe," she said. "But tell me—who made the best mashed potatoes in the world tonight?"

CHAPTER
10

◆ ◀ ◢ ◆

Stephanie tied her new apron around her waist. *Another night, another cooking challenge!* she thought.

It was Thursday, and she had to bake the three birthday cakes tonight. She was psyched after her successful mashed potatoes the night before. She was even eager to start cooking again!

She retied the hair scrunchie around her ponytail, then smoothed down the new apron. It was so cute! She felt a tiny pang of guilt at having spent money on an extra item. But worrying about it wasn't going to make her any more money! Anyway, her dad had lent her enough money to buy the rest of her catering groceries.

She wiped off the kitchen counter with a clean

sponge, then opened her notebook to Chef Thelma's recipe for Knock 'Em Dead Chocolate Cake. It sounded so good, she was going to make it for all three cakes!

She turned the kitchen radio to her favorite station, neatly lined up all her baking utensils, and gathered all the cake ingredients from the pantry.

She glanced at the page where it said "Preparation Time: 1 hour, 30 minutes."

Great, she thought. *It's seven-thirty now. I'll be done in time to finish my homework and still get to bed early. This catering stuff is a breeze!*

She took a deep breath and began to read through her recipe notes.

"In large bowl, combine cup of sugar, two cups flour, one tsp. baking powder, one tsp. baking soda." Luckily, she remembered that "tsp." meant teaspoon. She wasn't about to use *tablespoons* again!

She found a large mixing bowl in a cabinet over the fridge.

"Perfect. This bowl will hold three batches of batter, no problem. Tanner's Tasties is back in business!"

Stephanie tripled the butter and sugar and mixed them in the bowl. There was plenty of room left over.

Next it was time to add the eggs. She read the

recipe again. "Separate four eggs and mix the egg whites on high."

Stephanie took a small bowl out of the cabinet and began to separate the eggs, letting the egg whites fall into the dry cake mixture. She put the yolks in the small bowl. Not one broken! She was suddenly glad she'd paid attention in home economics class.

When all the eggs were separated, she began to mix the egg whites into the batter at high speed.

She took another look at the recipe as she continued to mix.

"Beat egg whites at high speed," she said, reading out loud. "Set egg whites aside for later and add egg yolks to cake mixture. . . . Oh, no! I was supposed to beat the egg whites by themselves!"

Quickly, she pulled the electric hand mixer out of the bowl. Only she forgot to turn it off first. Clumps of gooey batter flew all over the kitchen.

"Ahhh!" she cried helplessly. She reached for the Off button. Then she looked around the kitchen in dismay. There was batter everywhere!

D.J. hurried downstairs. She gaped in surprise when she found Stephanie scraping cake batter off the toaster.

"I heard a scream," D.J. said. She gazed around the kitchen. "What happened in here?"

Stephanie wiped a glop of batter off her forehead with the back of her hand. "It's this dumb recipe!" she wailed. "They tell you to do things after it's too late!"

D.J. leaned over and looked into the bowl. "Why is there so much stuff in here?" she asked.

"Because I'm tripling the recipe to make three cakes at one time," Stephanie explained.

"Oh, right," D.J. said. "It's a good thing we bought extra eggs."

"Extra eggs?" Stephanie stared at her sister.

"Sure. If you had to triple them."

"The eggs!" Stephanie groaned.

"Is something wrong?" D.J. asked.

"I forgot to triple the eggs!" Stephanie said. "The recipe said four eggs for one cake, but I'm making three cakes. I should have put in twelve eggs!" She dropped her head onto her hands.

D.J. stared. "This is really out of control, Stephanie. For something so important you should have paid more attention."

"Isn't there something we can do to fix this?" Stephanie wailed.

"I'm not sure," D.J. said. She peered at the mixing bowl. "Now, you said you put in four eggs?"

Stephanie bit her bottom lip. "Well, kind of," she said. "I put in four egg whites."

D.J. reread the recipe. "But you're supposed to set the whites aside and—"

"I know!" Stephanie replied in a panic. "I told you I goofed!"

D.J. took a deep breath. She marched over to the refrigerator. "Look, we have plenty more eggs," she told Stephanie.

"What are you going to do?" Stephanie asked nervously.

"*You're* going to start over again," D.J. said. "I'm going to watch to make sure you don't mess up." D.J. handed her the eggs.

Stephanie began the recipe one more time. This time she tripled the amount. And set the whites aside. D.J. watched her the whole time, scowling.

Finally, the cakes were ready to go in the oven.

"It's all yours from here," D.J. said with a yawn. "I still have some studying to do before I go to sleep. I'll tell Dad you won't be up much longer. Oh, and speaking of Dad, you'd better scrape the batter off the ceiling before he sees it in the morning."

D.J. went upstairs and Stephanie set the oven timer. She still needed to frost the cakes and write the messages on them with icing. The recipe said it took fifty minutes for the cakes to bake.

She yawned again and cleaned up all the icing.

Finally, she sank into a chair and rested her head on the kitchen table.

The next thing she knew, she was being woken by the timer. In a sleepy daze she took the cakes from the oven, set them on the counter, and waited for them to cool. Then she took out three cans of frosting and spread them on the cakes. She wrote the messages with the neon-colored icing.

"Yikes!" she mumbled, glancing at the clock. "It's after one A.M.! No wonder I'm so tired." It looked as though her homework was not going to get done tonight.

With a final yawn she finished in the kitchen, then climbed upstairs. She got ready for bed in the dark, being careful not to wake Michelle.

Finally, she crawled under her covers. *There's one good thing about tonight*, she told herself as she drifted off to sleep. *I learned never to bake three cakes at once again!*

CHAPTER
11

◆ ◢ ◣ ◆

"Stephanie!" Michelle's voice rang out. "I said, it's time to get up!"

Stephanie could barely open her eyes. It was the next morning, and Michelle was tugging on her arm.

Stephanie forced herself to sit up. "Did Dad leave for work yet?" she asked groggily.

"He's leaving now," Michelle told her.

"He can't!" Stephanie cried. "He has to take his cake with him!" She jumped out of bed, pulled on her robe, and ran downstairs. Danny was just walking out the door.

"Wait, Dad!" she called out. "I have the cake for you!"

"Oh, right! I almost forgot!" Danny said. He smiled at his daughter. "You're one great caterer, Stephanie Tanner! So organized too!" He handed her another five dollars.

Stephanie raced into the kitchen and pulled one of the cakes from the fridge. It was wrapped in aluminum foil and labeled CAKE FOR DAD. She handed it to her father.

"Thanks for remembering!" Danny said with a smile.

Stephanie laughed. "How could I forget? I was up all night baking it!"

Her father left for work and Stephanie raced back upstairs to get ready for school.

"So, why are you so tired today?" Darcy asked at lunch.

Stephanie tried to cover yet another yawn as she picked at her food. "I was up late baking cakes," she said sleepily. *Does the cafeteria have to be so loud?* she wondered to herself.

"Sorry you couldn't hang out with us," Allie told her.

"Well, that's okay. It was worth staying up late," Stephanie replied. "Because the cakes came out great."

"You know, Steph, you act like you don't want

to spend any time with us at all," Darcy complained.

"That's not true," Stephanie insisted. "It's just that I'm so busy these days. I shouldn't have agreed to swap cooking chores with everyone at home. I thought I needed the practice, but I didn't know how much work I'd have to do for this business."

Allie swallowed some juice. "Well, our offer to help on Sunday still stands," she said. "And you know, I have an awesome brownie recipe. You could borrow it for Michelle's bake sale. I've made it about a million times. And the brownies are always chewy." Allie's eyes began to shine. "I could give you lots of other pointers too. And I could—"

"Allie, please. It's okay," Stephanie said. "I've got it all under control."

Allie sighed. "Okay."

"We can hang out together just as soon as this weekend is over," Stephanie promised.

"Really?" Allie looked doubtful.

"Sure," Stephanie said. "Once Tanner's Tasties is off the ground, the business will practically run itself. I'll have lots of time then. Definitely."

After school Stephanie rushed home. *Why, oh, why, did I promise to cook dinner?* she thought. It was such a hassle.

Joey met her at the front door with a huge smile on his face. "Guess what?" he asked.

Stephanie looked at her watch. "What is it, Joey? I have a zillion things to do." She took off her jacket.

"I got you another job!" he announced excitedly.

"Another job?" She shook her head. "Forget it. I can't possibly take it," she said.

"But it's a dinner order! And guess how much money it's for?" Joey waited for her answer.

Stephanie shrugged. "I don't know, and I don't care, Joey. No matter how much it is, I absolutely can't take one more order."

"But it's for sixty dollars!" Joey exclaimed.

Stephanie stared at him in disbelief. "Sixty dollars?" She grabbed a piece of paper and a pencil and figured out the numbers.

Joey's sixty dollars, plus the five her dad just gave her for the cake, would repay Danny what he had lent her. And she would have forty-two dollars left over!

Counting money this way made her head ache! But she knew she could really use the extra amount. It was almost too good to be true!

"Yup," Joey said. "I was telling my friend Richie about your great mashed potatoes the other night. And about the delicious dinner last week. Richie said he could really use someone to make dinner for our big card game Saturday night. So I told him you'd take the job!"

Stephanie swallowed hard. "*Saturday* night?" she asked. "You mean tomorrow night?"

"Yup. Nothing fancy or anything, but you definitely have to make those amazing potatoes." Joey reached into his wallet and pulled out thirty dollars.

Stephanie stared at the crisp ten- and twenty-dollar bills. "Oh, sure, the amazing potatoes," she said. In the back of her mind she wondered how she was going to fit in another dinner—with all the cooking she had to do for Sunday.

Joey waved the thirty dollars. She reached for them.

"Okay," she said. "It's a deal. But I can't make a big, fancy dinner on such short notice. I'll just whip up some baked ziti and garlic bread."

"And mashed potatoes," Joey added.

Stephanie sighed. "Right. And mashed potatoes."

Joey smiled. "Excellent!"

"But you have to take me to the supermarket right away," Stephanie said, putting her jacket back on. "I won't be able to go at all tomorrow. In fact, I don't think I'll even be able to leave the kitchen tomorrow!"

Joey grabbed his car keys. "Okay, let's go," he said.

When they returned from the supermarket, Stephanie marched into the kitchen. Michelle and D.J. were doing homework at the kitchen table.

"Okay!" Stephanie cried. "Everyone out of the kitchen! Let's go! Hop to it!"

D.J. and Michelle looked up from their books.

"Uh-oh," Michelle said. "It's the Wicked Kitchen Queen."

Stephanie put the grocery bags down and walked over to the table. She closed Michelle's textbook.

"Very funny," Stephanie said. "But I mean it! You guys have to go. I need complete privacy and total quiet to concentrate! I have a lot of cooking to do!"

"But we're just reading," D.J. pointed out.

"D.J.!" Stephanie wailed. "Please! I can't work with all you people in here! I have to think! I need complete silence!"

Michelle gathered up her things. "Ever since you've become a chef you've become so . . . rude!"

She grabbed her books and stormed out of the kitchen.

"D.J.?" Stephanie pleaded.

D.J. sighed. "Fine. I'll leave too. But Michelle is right. You have become rude!"

As soon as they were gone, Stephanie pulled out her new cooking schedule.

"Okay," she said, reading out loud to herself. "There's a million things to be done. First . . . the sauce for the baked ziti. Then I can—"

She suddenly remembered dinner.

"Ugh!" She peered inside the refrigerator. "Hmmm, let's see. What's quick? What's easy?"

She noticed a package of bologna. Okay, so it wasn't exactly like cooking a real meal. But it would do.

Stephanie made eighteen bologna sandwiches. She opened a jar of pickles for a side dish.

Her father was the first one in the kitchen. He cringed when he saw the sandwiches stacked in the middle of the kitchen table.

"Stephanie," Danny said, "we really need to talk about your dinner menus for the family."

"I know, I know," Stephanie replied. "But tonight's the last night."

"I'm glad to hear that," Danny said. He paused.

"So, your business is going great. I guess I was wrong about how hard it was going to be."

"Yeah. I guess so," Stephanie said. She forced a laugh.

Danny clapped Stephanie on the back. "Well, you fooled me. Still, if you need any help, let me know. I'd be glad to do anything!"

"Why is everyone always telling me they can help?" Stephanie cried in exasperation. "Haven't I proved to you that I can do things by myself?"

"Easy, Steph. I didn't mean to insult you," Danny told her.

"Sorry, Dad," Stephanie apologized. She thought for a minute. "Actually, there is something you could do for me," she said.

"Anything, Steph! I can boil and broil and bake with the best of them!" Danny grinned at her.

"Not that kind of help," Stephanie told him. "I mean, letting my father cook for me wouldn't prove a thing—except that I couldn't run my own business."

"Well, I don't know if I agree with that," Danny said. "But tell me what I *can* do for you."

"Uh, after dinner," she began, "could you write down your recipe for your world-famous tomato sauce? I want to use it in the ziti."

"Of course!" Danny said. "Now can I tell every-one that dinner's ready?"

"Sure," Stephanie told him. She watched as the kitchen door swung shut behind her father.

Bologna sandwiches, she thought. *How low I have sunk in just one week!*

CHAPTER

12

◆ ◀ ◾ ◆

"What smells so good?" Joey asked. It was Saturday morning. Joey came into the kitchen on his way to get the morning paper.

Stephanie wiped her hands on her apron. "Brownies," she said. "I made them from scratch. And I made real homemade tomato sauce for the baked ziti," she said. "The kind that needs all day to cook."

"Boy, you've been busy. You must have gotten up early," Joey said.

"At the crack of dawn," Stephanie said. She let out a heavy sigh of relief. "But it was worth it. I'm finally ahead of schedule. Now I have the whole day to work on the other stuff—your card game dinner, Darcy and Allie's dinner, and Amy's birthday party."

"I'm impressed, Steph," Joey said.

"Are those my brownies?" Michelle called out, rushing into the kitchen. She peered into the oven.

"Yes, but they're not ready yet. I made four dozen for your bake sale. Even though you called me rude."

Michelle blushed. "I'm sorry, Steph," she said. "I didn't mean it. You're the best sister in the world!"

Stephanie folded her arms across her chest and smirked. "I know," she said. "Not to mention the best cook in the world! Wait till you taste the brownies. I think they're going to be great. The batter tasted excellent!"

Michelle pointed to the enormous pot on top of the stove. "What's that for?" she asked.

"It's for the ziti noodles," Stephanie told her. "I borrowed the pot from our neighbor, Mrs. Roselli. I used our big pot for the tomato sauce and didn't have another for the ziti."

"How much sauce are you making?" Michelle asked.

"A lot!" Stephanie told her. "I decided to make all the ziti platters at once. One for Joey's card game, one for Amy Lodge's birthday party, and two more platters for my dinner with Allie's and Darcy's families tomorrow night."

"That's using your keen business sense again!" D.J. called.

Everyone looked up to see D.J. coming down the stairs. "Saving time and money—nice going. I'm going to mention that in my economics project." She glanced around the kitchen. "Boy, it's so much calmer in here today! You really have everything under control, Steph. Hey, I'm going to get my camcorder and get this all on tape!"

That didn't bother Stephanie one bit. In fact, she was glad D.J. was going to tape her working this morning. She really did have things under control. The brownies were baking, she'd already made the garlic bread loaves and wrapped them in foil to be cooked later, and the sauce for the ziti was simmering on the stove. Things couldn't be going more smoothly.

D.J. filmed while Stephanie chopped vegetables. She pretended that she was hosting her own cooking show.

"Today, I, Chef Steph, world-famous chef and super-smart and savvy businesswoman, will show you how to chop tomatoes," she said in a silly accent. "First, you get a knife. Then you get some tomatoes. Then ... you chop them. Thank you.

Thank you very much. See you tomorrow, same time, same channel.''

D.J. cracked up. "You're pathetic, Chef Steph," she joked.

When the salad was finished, Stephanie checked her cooking schedule wall chart. "Time to start boiling the water for the ziti," she said.

D.J. pointed the camera at the chart. "Wow, Steph! This chart is amazing! You've even color-coded the different pots and pans to use!"

Stephanie grinned.

"That *is* impressive!" a voice behind her said.

Stephanie turned to see her uncle Jesse. "Thanks, Uncle Jesse."

"One problem though," he said. "Uh, D.J.—could you excuse us for a minute?" Jesse asked.

D.J. turned off the video camera. "Okay." She shrugged. "I have lots of other work I could be doing anyway."

As soon as D.J. was gone, Jesse quickly checked to make sure no one else was around.

"What's wrong, Uncle Jesse?" Stephanie asked. "I'm sure I have everything under control."

"The dinner for Becky," Jesse whispered. "It isn't on the chart. You didn't forget, did you?"

Stephanie felt her face get hot. She *had* forgotten!

"Forget?" she said with a nervous laugh. "Of

course not! I, uh, didn't put it on the chart because I didn't want Becky to see it. That would ruin the surprise, silly!"

Jesse smiled in relief. "Oh! Good thinking, Steph!"

Jesse left the kitchen whistling.

"Now what will I do?" Stephanie asked herself in dismay. She made a mental note to remember to plan the romantic Japanese dinner for Jesse and Becky later that night. Luckily, she was already ahead of schedule. So she could still prepare it tomorrow morning.

Now to get back to work! she told herself.

When the salad was done and the ziti noodles were finished cooking, Stephanie began to make up the ziti platters. First she layered the pans with some sauce. Then she put in a layer of pasta. Then she covered the pasta with soft ricotta cheese. Then some more sauce, and then a layer of shredded mozzarella cheese. She did this twice in each pan, and by two o'clock there were four big ziti platters baking in the oven.

Stephanie set the timer for an hour and a half and wiped her hands on her apron. Then she gazed around the kitchen.

It was a total mess.

"Yuck. There's tomato sauce all over the place!" Stephanie exclaimed out loud.

She grabbed a sponge and began to clean. She couldn't believe the places where the bright red sauce had splattered. There was even sauce dripping down the crack behind the stove!

At three o'clock Stephanie was still scraping sauce off the floor, when she heard strange chewing and slurping noises. She looked up and when she saw what it was, she screamed. Comet, the family dog, was on the kitchen table, devouring a pan of brownies.

"Comet!" she shouted. "No! Bad dog!"

Comet stopped at the sound of Stephanie's voice, but not until after knocking a second pan of brownies over, onto the kitchen floor.

"Noooo!" Stephanie wailed. "Comet! How could you do this to me?"

Comet slinked away with a whiskerful of brownie crumbs.

Stephanie moaned in despair. What was she going to do?

She'd promised Michelle she'd make four dozen brownies. Now she was going to have to make two dozen more!

Stephanie grumbled to herself as she opened the

pantry and pulled out the ingredients for brownies. Still grumbling, she began mixing all over again.

"Flour, baking powder, and sugar," she growled, grabbing the "S" canister and dumping it into the mixing bowl. "This baking stuff is really beginning to bug me!"

It was after five o'clock before the new brownies were done. Stephanie set them out to cool on the kitchen counter. She sat down to catch her breath.

"Hi, Steph!" Michelle appeared in the kitchen.

Stephanie jumped, feeling guilty. "Michelle! What do you want?" she nearly shouted.

Michelle frowned. "You don't have to yell. I just wanted to taste one of my brownies."

"They're not cool yet," Stephanie snapped.

"They've been sitting there all day," Michelle pointed out. "How could they still be hot?"

No way could Stephanie admit she had to make the brownies over. "Uh, it's because the oven was extra hot today," she fibbed.

Michelle gave her a strange look. "Oh, well," she said. "I can wait."

"Okay, but wait quietly," Stephanie told her. She glanced around the kitchen. "I feel like I'm forgetting something," she muttered. "But what?"

Stephanie glanced through her schedule notes.

"Let's see . . . ziti . . . salad . . . wait! I remember! The mashed potatoes for the card game!"

She reached for the bag of potatoes on the counter and grabbed a potato peeler. She pulled a chair up to the garbage can and got ready to peel. But when she removed a potato from the bag, she cried out in disgust.

"Eewww! This potato is bad!" She dropped the moldy potato immediately into the garbage. She dumped out the rest.

"They're all bad! What am I going to do?" Stephanie stared at the rotten potatoes in dismay.

"Stay calm?" Michelle asked.

"Thanks. You're a big help," Stephanie grumbled. "I have to do something!"

"So, get someone to take you to the store," Michelle suggested. "Buy more potatoes."

"I'll still need time to peel them, cook them, and mash them," Stephanie told her. "And there's not enough time now."

She went to the pantry. "This will just have to do," she said. She pulled a box of instant mashed potatoes from the pantry and began to mix the ingredients.

They'll never know the difference, she told herself. She followed the instructions on the box. In minutes she had a big bowl of instant mashed potatoes.

"See?" she said to Michelle. "Problem solved. Chef Stephanie is on the case!"

She remembered to add some paprika, just like she'd done the other night. She covered the bowl. "Just like homemade!"

"And just in time," Michelle said. She pointed at the clock. It was a little before six. "You need a bath!"

"Guess again, Michelle," Stephanie said. She glanced down at herself. She was covered with red sauce and brownie batter. Her face and neck were hot and sticky.

"I don't have time to change or shower," she said.

Stephanie quickly began to load the food into Joey's car.

D.J. appeared, carrying her video camera. Stephanie noticed that D.J. looked crisp and neat, as always. Her hair was combed into a smooth ponytail and her outfit was spotless.

"D.J., can you turn that darn camera off and help me carry this stuff?" Stephanie said. "This ziti platter is heavy!"

D.J. turned off her camera. She took the garlic bread loaves out from under Stephanie's arm.

"Aren't you going to thank me?" she asked.

"Thank you," Stephanie mumbled. Then she

yelled back toward the house. "Joey! Come on! We have to get to Richie's house right away! I have to reheat the ziti and the garlic bread!"

Joey hurried outside. "Is that what you're wearing?" he asked.

Stephanie looked down at her clothes. She pulled off the apron and tossed it onto the front steps.

"Michelle!" she yelled. Michelle appeared in the doorway. "Can you throw my apron in the hamper?" she asked.

Michelle shot her a dirty look. "For someone who doesn't want any help, you sure seem needy."

"Sorry," Stephanie said. She took a deep breath. "I'm just in a hurry, that's all. Thank you all for helping me. Now, Joey ... step on it!"

Stephanie jumped into the passenger seat and Joey pulled out of the driveway.

"Wait!" she suddenly yelled.

Joey slammed on the brakes. "What? What is it?"

Stephanie opened the car door and jumped out. "The mashed potatoes! I almost forgot them!"

"And why don't you bring out the cake for my friend Samantha too?" Joey suggested. "We can drop it off now. Sam's house is on the way to Richie's."

"Why not," Stephanie grumbled.

She tore into the house and grabbed the bowl of mashed potatoes. She rechecked her list to make sure she had everything. She ran back out to the car.

"Okay for real this time. Now, step on it!"

At Richie's house, Stephanie took over the kitchen. "You guys stay in the dining room," she commanded. "Dinner will be ready shortly."

Richie and his poker buddies exchanged looks. "Uh, Stephanie, what about the appetizers?"

Stephanie swallowed hard. "The appetizers?" she asked.

Richie looked at Joey. "Didn't you tell her we usually have some appetizers before the game?"

Joey bit his thumbnail. "Uh, I kind of forgot to mention it," he said.

Stephanie's eyes widened. "You forgot to mention it? That's a pretty big thing to forget to mention, Joey!" she said.

"Uh, so, does that mean there aren't any appetizers?" Richie asked. He sounded disappointed.

Stephanie thought for a moment. She couldn't let a big job go sour. It was bad for business. She ushered Joey and Richie and the others out of the kitchen.

"Of course there are appetizers!" she said. "I

have a batch of great stuff already made back at home. I'll just have my assistant pick them up!"

Joey stared at her strangely.

Stephanie ignored him. When she was sure they were all out of earshot, she picked up the phone.

"D.J.!" she cried. "Thank goodness you're home!"

"Stephanie, what are you doing? Aren't you supposed to be working?"

"D.J., stop talking and listen!" Stephanie ordered. "There isn't much time. Joey forgot to tell me about the appetizers, so I need you to run to the store and get some!"

"You what?"

"Please, oh, please, oh, please! D.J., I really need you to do this for me!" she begged. "It's my first big job! If I blow it, word will get out that I'm a lousy caterer and Tanner's Tasties will be history! So will Uncle Jesse and Aunt Becky's CD player. And so will your economics project!" she added.

D.J. sighed. "Okay, what should I get?"

"Oh, D.J.! You're the best sister in the universe!"

"Yeah, yeah," D.J. replied. "Just tell me what to get."

Stephanie thought for a minute. "Okay, go to the frozen food section and pick up some pizza bagels, some chicken nuggets, and some cheese puffs."

"But those are so expensive!" D.J. pointed out. "Stephanie, remember you don't have extra money to spend."

"Will you stop worrying about money? Just get them!"

"But—" D.J. began to protest.

"D.J.! Just go! Don't worry! Once I get back on track, all this cooking and baking is really going to pay off! I promise! We'll be rolling in, er, dough!"

CHAPTER

13

◆ ◀ ▸ ◆

Ding. Ding. Ding. Ding. Ding.

Stephanie woke with a jolt. "Turn off the oven!" she cried out in confusion. "The brownies are burning!"

She gazed around her bedroom and rubbed her eyes.

Ding. Ding. Ding. Ding.

She glanced over at her nightstand and laughed. It was her alarm clock ringing, not the oven! But the smile disappeared from her face when she remembered what day it was. Sunday. The big day. She had so much to do! There wasn't a moment to waste.

With one final yawn she hopped out of bed, threw on her robe, and ran down to the kitchen.

Downstairs, Michelle was already getting ready to leave for her softball game and bake sale. Stephanie thrust the shoe boxes filled with brownies at her sister.

Michelle lifted the lids of both boxes. "How come these brownies look different than those?" Michelle asked. "These look so soft and chewy and those are so . . . uh, flat."

"Don't worry about it," Stephanie told her. "I had a little problem with half the brownies yesterday and I had to do them over again."

"What happened?" Michelle asked.

"Ask your dog what happened," Stephanie replied.

Michelle's eyes widened. "Comet ate them?" she asked.

"Two dozen of them," Stephanie told her. "Now, shouldn't you be going?"

Michelle left through the back door, shaking her head.

Stephanie glanced around the kitchen. She was really beginning to get sick of this room. It was the last place she felt like being right now. But she didn't have a choice. Amy Lodge's birthday party was less than three hours away. There was money to make and work to be done.

Yawning, Stephanie checked her wall chart. She

had to thaw a frozen platter of ziti for Amy's birthday party and chop some more garlic for the garlic bread. Plus, there was the vermicelli to make for Allie's mom, and the ratatouille to prepare for Darcy's father.

D.J. came downstairs a little while later. She was still in her robe and pajamas. "So how did it go last night?" she asked.

"Don't ask," Stephanie mumbled. She pulled a frozen baked ziti out of the freezer and set it on the counter. It was harder than a rock.

"What do you mean, 'Don't ask,' " D.J. said. "Didn't they love your ziti?"

"Yup. The ziti wasn't the problem," she said. "Actually, that was the only thing good about the dinner."

"I don't understand," D.J. said.

Stephanie sighed. "Where should I start? Okay, the pizza bagels burned. The chicken nuggets were taking too long, so I nuked them in the microwave. Then they came out rubbery. The cheese puffs didn't puff, they exploded, squirting cheese all over Richie's oven which I had to clean. And the mashed potatoes . . . well, let's just say that they noticed they were instant and not homemade."

D.J. looked puzzled. "What do you mean, 'instant'?"

"Can we keep this off the record?" Stephanie asked.

"Sure," D.J. told her.

"Well," Stephanie went on, "the potatoes were all rotten, and I didn't have time to get more, so I made the instant kind instead."

"Oh, Steph," D.J. said sympathetically. "And they could really tell?"

Stephanie nodded. "Right away. Joey still isn't talking to me."

"Look at the bright side," D.J. told her. "You still got paid."

"Not exactly."

D.J.'s eyes widened. "What do you mean?"

"Richie paid me half," Stephanie admitted. "He said he would have paid more, but since the garlic bread fell on the floor . . ."

"The garlic bread fell on the floor?" D.J. asked.

"It was sort of an accident. But it kind of got kicked around a bit. And then his dog choked on a piece of garlic bread."

"So, how much money do you have left?" D.J. asked.

"I have no idea!" Stephanie exclaimed. "I'm so confused, I can't figure it out. And right now I really have to get organized for the birthday party this afternoon. At least this won't go into your project, right?"

D.J. shook her head. "Stephanie, I have to include it in my presentation. It's all part of the business."

Stephanie groaned. She thought hard for a minute. "Actually, my first catering order was for Amy Lodge's birthday party. Couldn't you just pretend the card game dinner never happened? You can still record the results of the birthday party for your project."

"Yeah, okay." D.J. frowned. "I'll go get my notes."

D.J. ran upstairs and Stephanie immediately got busy. She placed the dish of ziti high up on a kitchen shelf so Comet couldn't get at it. She began chopping garlic.

At a quarter to twelve Stephanie packed the food for the party. The frozen ziti hadn't thawed at all.

Oh, well. No problem. She'd stick the dish in the oven as soon as she got to the Lodges'.

Mrs. Lodge was waiting at the door when Stephanie and D.J. showed up at noon. D.J. had decided to tag along and film the party for her project.

"Deej, do you have to film absolutely everything?" Stephanie asked. "I really need to concentrate on this party. The camera is so distracting."

"Pretend I'm not here," D.J. replied.

"Ha!" Stephanie scoffed. "Like that's possible when you're pointing a camera in my face every second!"

In the Lodges' kitchen, the first thing Stephanie did was stick the frozen ziti in the oven. Mrs. Lodge had asked her to serve lunch around one-thirty.

Next, she began slicing the garlic bread. D.J. moved in close with the camera, filming as Stephanie sliced each piece.

"D.J.! Do you really need a close-up of the garlic bread?" Stephanie complained.

D.J. put down the camera. "I guess not," she said. "Maybe I'll go down to the basement and film the party for Mrs. Lodge."

"Good idea!" Stephanie replied.

Finally, the bread was sliced and ready. Stephanie checked on the baked ziti. She pulled on oven mitts and opened the oven door. Something was wrong.

She slid out the oven shelf and touched the ziti. It was still frozen solid!

"That's impossible!" Stephanie cried. She pulled off her mitts and touched the inside of the oven. "It isn't even warm yet!"

In a panic, she checked the oven's temperature dial. It was still on Off.

She'd forgotten to turn the oven on!

Stephanie took a deep breath. *Okay, whatever you do, don't panic!* she told herself. *Just turn the oven on now, and the kiddies will just have to wait a bit longer for their lunch.*

She turned the oven up to 400 degrees and shut the oven door. Then she had a second thought. If the oven was even hotter, maybe the ziti would thaw faster. So she turned up the oven thermostat to 500 degrees.

That should do it, she thought.

Downstairs, D.J. was filming Amy and her friends as they played musical chairs. They seemed to be having a great time. When they saw Stephanie, they all stopped playing and ran over.

"Is lunch ready yet?" Amy asked.

"Yeah! We're starving!" another little girl exclaimed.

Stephanie smiled at the children. "Twenty more minutes!" she told them. "So why don't we play another game while we wait? How about Twister?"

The kids all cheered.

"Gee, Steph," D.J. teased. "I wonder why you

didn't start a business running children's parties? You're pretty good with kids."

"Don't even joke about it," Stephanie told her.

A half hour later Stephanie left the Twister game to go check on the ziti. As soon as she walked into the kitchen, she noticed a funny smell.

Then she saw a tiny stream of smoke coming from the oven

"Oh, no!" she gasped, racing toward the oven. She pulled open the oven door. More smoke poured out. Choking, she yanked out the ziti and dropped the dish onto the counter. The top of the casserole was completely black. She stuck a knife into it.

Maybe I can slice off the burnt part, she thought. *Oh, no! I don't believe this!* The middle of the casserole was still frozen solid!

A second later the Lodges' smoke detector went off. Mrs. Lodge and the kids raced upstairs.

"Fire! Fire!" the kids all shouted.

"Uh, no! There's no fire!" Stephanie called out. She grabbed a dish towel and began flapping it at the smoke detector until the alarm stopped.

"It's just some smoke. The, uh, ziti burned a little," Stephanie explained.

Mrs. Lodge stared at the blackened mound of food. "A little?" she asked.

"I'm so sorry, Mrs. Lodge!" Stephanie said. "I spent so much time on this ziti! I made my own sauce and everything! It just wouldn't thaw, so I turned up the heat, and . . . I'm so sorry." She felt a tear slip down her cheek.

Mrs. Lodge shook her head. "Don't cry, Stephanie. These things happen," she said wearily. "I'll just order something for the kids, I guess." She thought for a minute.

"I know," Mrs. Lodge continued. "Why don't you go downstairs and serve the cake now. The kids will love having dessert first."

"Well, what about their lunch?" Stephanie asked.

"I'll have lunch delivered after the cake." She dialed a number.

Stephanie felt like the biggest loser ever. She pulled twenty-five dollars from her pocket. "Here, Mrs. Lodge. For the take-out food," she said. She held out the bills.

Mrs. Lodge looked at the money, then at Stephanie. "Stephanie, you keep the money," Mrs. Lodge said gently. "We can still eat your garlic bread. And the birthday cake."

Stephanie smiled gratefully. "Thank you so much, Mrs. Lodge. And really, I'm so sorry!"

"Well, these things do happen." Mrs. Lodge

sighed and picked up the phone. "Hello? Luigi's? Do you have ziti for twelve?" she asked.

Stephanie carried the cake downstairs. Her first catered party wasn't going at all the way she'd planned it. But at least the kids would love her birthday cake.

Stephanie walked home from the Lodges' with her head hung low. "Tanner's Tasties is the biggest mistake I've ever made in my life. Where did I get the dumb idea that I could run a catering business?" she asked.

D.J. didn't answer.

"I know, I know," Stephanie answered instead. "I cooked one really good meal and got carried away. Everything I've touched since then has turned into a major disaster."

"Your garlic bread was pretty good ... especially with Luigi's ziti," D.J. told her.

"Ha! I probably couldn't cater a cold cereal convention," Stephanie said.

"You're not a bad cook," D.J. said. "Remember those great lamb chops you made?" she reminded her.

"And those mashed potatoes," Stephanie added.

"Right!" D.J. said. "Those were excellent. You are a good cook. It's just that ..."

Stephanie gazed up. "It's just what?" she asked.

D.J. took a deep breath. "Well, it's just that you may be an excellent cook . . . but you're a rotten caterer."

Stephanie groaned. "So what am I going to do?" she asked.

"I think it's time to hang up your apron," D.J. said.

"You mean close Tanner's Tasties . . . forever?" Stephanie asked.

D.J. nodded.

"You're right," Stephanie said. There was just one problem.

How could she pay for Uncle Jesse and Aunt Becky's CD player now?

CHAPTER
14

◆ ◀ ◾ ◆

Danny was in the living room when they got home from the Lodges'.

"So, honey, how was the party?" Danny asked. "Oh, and before I forget, I have some money from Michelle for you. She said your brownies were a big hit!"

"Really?" Stephanie took the money from her father, but she couldn't look him in the eye. She was too embarrassed to tell him what had happened at the Lodges'.

"Stephanie?" Danny asked again. "The party? How did it go?"

"It was . . . *well done!*" Stephanie joked.

"I don't follow . . ." Danny said.

Stephanie took a deep breath, then explained. "I burned the ziti," she blurted out. "In fact, there was a small fire. It sort of set off the smoke detector."

Danny winced. "I'm sorry, sweetheart."

Stephanie shook her head. "It was awful. I nearly ruined the party. Just like I ruined the eggplant Parmesan the other night. And the chili!" She groaned and fell onto the sofa. "I am *never*, ever cooking again!" she proclaimed.

Danny grinned. "Well, before you swear off cooking forever, I think you should know something."

Stephanie looked up. "What's that?" she asked.

"Allie and Darcy are here," Danny said. "They're waiting for you in the kitchen."

Stephanie stared at him blankly. Then she pulled herself up from the sofa and trudged into the kitchen.

"What are *you* guys doing here?" she asked.

"Well, we were in the neighborhood," Darcy began.

"And we thought we'd stop by to see how the dinner was going," Allie finished.

"Well, it's *not* going," Stephanie told them. "Not yet anyway. I just got back from my second catering job of the weekend." Stephanie tried to sound like a successful businesswoman in front of her friends. "Now, if you'll excuse me, I'll get started on tonight's meal."

Stephanie waited for Darcy and Allie to leave, but her friends didn't move. Why were they looking at her strangely?

Stephanie reached for her apron, but put it back as soon as she saw the big food stains from *this* morning's cooking.

"Listen," she said hastily. "I'd love to sit and chat—but then your dinner might be late."

Allie stepped forward. "Stephanie, we heard everything you told your dad."

Stephanie's fake look of confidence faded. "Everything?" she asked.

Allie and Darcy nodded.

Stephanie cringed. "So—go ahead—tell me 'I told you so.' You never thought I could do it without help. And you were right."

"That's not true," Allie said. "We were really impressed by how hard you were working! We just missed you."

"Right," Darcy agreed. "And we felt kind of bad because we were having fun and you were working all the time."

"Really? You really felt bad?" Stephanie asked.

"Yeah. And we still want to help. It could be fun," Allie said.

"That's why we're here. To give it one more shot," Darcy added.

Stephanie bit her lip. "Wow, you guys. I missed you too! And right now I'll take all the help I can get!"

She reached out and hugged her friends.

"So, did you really set off the smoke alarm?" Allie asked.

Stephanie nodded. "Yup!" She let out a giggle. "And I think I've lost more money than I ever made. Let's face it—I'm probably the worst caterer in the history of the world!"

"Not anymore," Allie said with a grin. "Just tell us what to do. We are your kitchen slaves."

Stephanie rubbed her hands together. "Okay, you asked for it! Let's see . . . first, I have to find some way to defrost these rock-solid ziti platters." She knocked one of the platters with a spoon to show her friends just how frozen they were.

"Whoa!" Allie said. "They're like glaciers!"

"Wait a minute. We're having ziti for dinner?" Darcy asked. "But that wasn't on our list."

"I know," Stephanie told her, "but I couldn't make any of those dishes on your list. Look at my vermicelli!" She pulled the dish of pasta out of the fridge.

Allie lifted the cover and stared at the gloppy stuff inside. "That doesn't look right," she said.

"No kidding," Stephanie said. She pulled the pasta box out from the pantry cabinet. "This is what the vermicelli was supposed to look like," she said, pointing to the picture on the box.

Darcy laughed. "It looks more like the picture on this box," she said, holding up a box of Cream of Wheat.

"Ha-ha," Stephanie said. "And do you want to see your dad's ratatouille, Darcy?"

Darcy chuckled. "I don't know, do I?"

Stephanie pulled another casserole dish from the fridge and held it open.

Allie and Darcy peered inside. "Yuck!" they both cried.

"Is it supposed to be all brown and globby like that?" Allie asked.

"Not exactly," Darcy said with a grimace. She turned to Stephanie. "Baked ziti will be fine."

"Baked ziti sounds perfect," Allie agreed.

"I thought you might feel that way," Stephanie said. She trashed the vermicelli and the ratatouille, then went back to the frozen ziti platters. "So . . . any ideas?" she asked.

"How about the microwave?" Darcy suggested.

"But they're in aluminum pans," Allie pointed out. "I don't think you can put aluminum in a microwave oven."

"But what if we took the ziti out of the pans and put it in a glass dish?" Darcy suggested.

Stephanie and Allie exchanged looks.

"Might work," Allie said. "Let's try it!"

"Okay. I guess we have time." Stephanie glanced at the clock. It was after five—almost time for Darcy's and Allie's families to arrive.

She felt a burst of panic. "Oh, no," she said. "It's later than I realized! We've got to hurry! Allie, you peel the pans off the ziti. Darcy, you take out some cheese and crackers for our parents to snack on—it will buy us some time. I'll start making the salad!"

The girls worked quietly in the kitchen. Allie came up with the idea of holding the frozen ziti under hot running water to loosen it from the pan. The only problem was, it also made the top of the ziti soggy.

"Well, maybe it'll dry off in the microwave," Stephanie said hopefully. She stuffed the slightly soggy ziti into a big glass dish and stuck it in the microwave oven.

"Time check!" she called out a little while later.

Darcy glanced at the kitchen clock. "Five forty-five!" she replied. "Boy, this catering stuff is harder than I thought!"

"How's the ziti doing, Allie?" Stephanie asked. "Dinner is supposed to be ready soon."

Allie stopped the microwave and checked the ziti. "Good news and bad news," she replied. "The good news is it's not frozen anymore."

"Excellent!" Stephanie exclaimed.

"The bad news," Allie went on, "is it doesn't look so good." She lifted the dish so Stephanie could see. The ziti noodles had gone from soggy to overcooked. And the cheese and sauce were all watery.

"Oh, gross!" Darcy said with a look of disgust. "We can't eat that!"

Stephanie began to panic. "But we have to eat it!" she exclaimed. "That's all we have!"

Allie shook her head. "Stephanie, we can't serve this stuff. Look at it!"

"But what are we going to do?" Stephanie cried.

"Start over," Darcy suggested. "Make new ziti platters."

"How long will that take?" Allie asked. Both girls looked at Stephanie.

"About an hour," Stephanie told them. "And your folks are supposed to be here in fifteen minutes."

She thought it over. It wasn't such a bad idea. She could serve the garlic bread and the salad while the ziti baked. "Okay," she sighed. "Let's make more. But we have to work fast!"

She raced to the stove and turned it on. Then she found a pot for cooking the pasta. She was filling it with water when she heard the doorbell ring. A moment later her father came in from the living room. He had a troubled look on his face.

"Uh, Stephanie," he said uncomfortably. "You'd better come out here right away. There's someone here to see you."

Stephanie left the pot in the sink and went into the living room. Allie and Darcy followed close behind. Stephanie frowned. Mrs. Lodge was at the front door. And she didn't look happy.

"Uh, hi, Mrs. Lodge," Stephanie said nervously. "What's up?"

Mrs. Lodge held little Amy's arm up for Stephanie to see. "Look!" she cried, rolling up Amy's sleeve. "Look what your birthday cake has done to poor Amy!"

Stephanie grimaced. Amy's arm was covered with a red, blotchy rash! "My birthday cake did that?" she asked.

"Yes! I told you Amy was allergic to chocolate!" Mrs. Lodge replied. "How could you make a chocolate cake for her birthday? I should never have let you serve it by yourself! I didn't even know it was chocolate because you covered it with all that neon-colored frosting. And it took a while for this rash to appear. But now look at it. And it keeps getting worse! Poor Amy is scratching like crazy!"

"Ow, Mommy, my feet itch too!" Amy wailed.

Stephanie felt terrible. "I'm so sorry, Amy," she said. "I forgot about your allergy!" She turned to Mrs. Lodge. "How long will the rash last?"

"Several days," Mrs. Lodge answered. "And now I have to keep her home from school."

Stephanie swallowed hard. She dug into her pocket and pulled out twenty-five dollars—again.

"Here," she said, handing the money to Mrs. Lodge. "I'm really sorry. About everything. The ziti, the cake, the rash . . . everything."

This time Mrs. Lodge accepted the money. She headed out the door with little Amy in tow. Stephanie closed the front door and leaned against it. "This can't be happening," she said.

There was another knock at the door. Stephanie opened it to find a woman she'd never seen before standing on the front stoop.

"Why, Kelly!" Danny exclaimed. "What are you doing here? It's so nice to see you!" He turned to the group. "This is Kelly, from my office."

Kelly was carrying a large plate covered in foil. "I'm, um, sorry to bother you at home, Danny," Kelly began. "It's just that . . . how could you have played such a cruel joke on me?" Her eyes filled with tears.

Danny seemed confused. "Joke? What are you talking about?" he asked.

"The cake for my engagement!" Kelly answered. "How could you? My fiancé was so upset when he saw it. I was never so humiliated!"

"I don't understand," Danny said. "What's wrong with the cake?"

Kelly pulled back the foil. "Dump the Jerk" read the message on the cake. "Is that supposed to be funny?" Kelly asked.

Danny gaped at the cake,.

Stephanie gulped. She'd given her father the wrong cake to take to the office engagement party! She gulped again. That meant . . .

The phone rang and Joey jumped up to answer it.

"Samantha? Hi, how are—what? Samantha, hold on. I can't understand what you're . . . huh? The cake? No, Samantha, I wasn't pulling a joke on you, I swear! . . . I'm so sorry."

Joey covered the mouthpiece and glared at Stephanie. "You gave Samantha a cake that said

'Congratulations on Your Engagement'? I told you the cake was to cheer her up after her boyfriend dumped her!"

Stephanie covered her face with her hands. "This is the worst moment of my entire life!"

"Uh, don't look now, Steph," Darcy warned her. "But I think the *worst* moment is about to get *terrible*."

A crowd of people suddenly appeared at the front door.

"Does Stephanie Tanner live here?" an angry-looking man demanded.

Danny stepped forward. "Yes, she does," he said nervously. "But can I help you?"

A young woman stepped forward. She was holding her son's hand. In her other hand she held a brownie. "My son plays in the softball league with Michelle. We bought these brownies today from the bake sale, and they're horrible! We want our money back!"

Stephanie's jaw nearly hit the floor.

"A buck fifty apiece for this garbage?" another man yelled. "I've never tasted anything so disgusting in my life! I want my money back too!"

"So do I!" shouted another.

Stephanie was beginning to feel dizzy. "But . . .

but those brownies were good," she said. "I tasted them myself! They were delicious!"

"We all want our money back!" the first man said. "What did you do, put salt in them instead of sugar?"

"Of course not. That's ridiculous!" Stephanie scoffed. "I can tell the difference between sugar and salt."

"Oh, really? Taste this brownie. Then tell me how delicious it is!" The woman handed Stephanie the brownie.

Stephanie took a bite and began to gag. "That . . . that's terrible!" she said, spitting it out. "But that couldn't be one of my brownies. I tasted them—"

Wait a minute! She suddenly realized—she had never tasted the *second* batch of brownies—the ones she'd baked after Comet devoured the first.

She spun around and ran into the kitchen. Darcy and Allie followed her. Stephanie flung open the cabinet. There were the canisters. "F" for the flour, "S" for the sugar, and "S"—for the salt!

"Oh, no!" Stephanie groaned. "I don't believe it!"

"What happened, Stephanie? What did you do?" Allie asked.

Stephanie took a deep breath. She faced her

friends. "I was in such a hurry. I grabbed the container marked "S"—and used salt instead of sugar! How could I have been so stupid?"

Allie and Darcy exchanged a look of disbelief. Luckily, neither of them said a word.

Stephanie slowly walked back into the living room. She reached into her pocket and took out all the money she had left from Tanner's Tasties. She divided it among the angry customers. When the last customer was gone, she had six dollars left to her name.

"Easy come, easy go," she said, closing the door.

Danny put his arm around her shoulders. "Stephanie, I'm sorry this had to happen, but perhaps you've learned a valuable lesson from all this?"

Stephanie rolled her eyes. "Yes, Dad. I learned that a paper route might be a better way to earn money."

Danny smiled. "No, really, Stephanie. The valuable lesson is that sometimes you can't do everything yourself. Promise me one thing." Danny squeezed her shoulder.

"What's that, Dad?" Stephanie asked.

"From now on, if you're in over your head, you'll ask for help! From me or D.J. or . . ."

"Me!" Allie chimed in.

"Or me!" Darcy added.

Stephanie grinned and nodded. "Yeah, okay." She sank down on the sofa. "Boy, I really messed up this time."

"Look at the bright side," Darcy told her. "The worst is over."

Allie nodded. "Right. I mean, nothing else could possibly go wrong."

Just then Michelle came down the stairs. She frowned and lifted her head, sniffing. "Hey, guys," she said. "What's burning?"

CHAPTER
15

◆ ◀ ◆ ◆

Stephanie raced into the kitchen with everyone following close behind. Smoke was pouring from the stove top.

"Not another fire!" she cried.

"What is it?" Allie asked. "What's burning?"

Stephanie grabbed an oven mitt and ran to the stove. "It's . . . it's . . . the salad!" she admitted.

In a flash she grabbed the wooden salad bowl and tossed it into the sink. She turned on the cold water. The bowl and the hot salad sizzled under the running water.

"You burned salad?" Allie asked.

"You burned salad?" Darcy repeated.

Stephanie hung her head. She was more embarrassed than she'd ever been in her life. She'd burned the salad. How pathetic was that?

Suddenly, Darcy began to giggle. Then Allie joined in, and soon everyone was laughing.

Everyone except Stephanie.

Stephanie just stared at them in disbelief. How could they laugh at her? Couldn't they see how humiliating this all was?

"Stephanie!" Allie gasped, trying to catch her breath. "You must be the only person in history who ever managed to burn a salad!"

Stephanie tried to fight it, but soon a tiny smile crept across her face. It blossomed into a grin. Finally, she burst out laughing.

"How in the world did you manage this, Steph?" Danny asked.

"It was easy," Stephanie told him. "I chopped the salad vegetables next to the stove. Then I put the salad bowl *on* the stove—because there was no place else to put it. Then, when we were ready to boil more ziti, I turned the wrong flame on. I didn't realize I turned it on under the salad bowl—and then, well, you know, Kelly came to the door, and you know the rest."

"Yes, but do you realize what this means?" Allie asked.

Stephanie stared at her. "What?"

"You were right all along," Allie replied.

"I don't get it," Stephanie said.

Darcy began to chuckle. "I do! There was no place else to put the salad because Allie and I were in here helping. Don't you see?"

Stephanie was still baffled. She shook her head.

"There were too many of us in the kitchen trying to cook," Darcy told her with a wide grin. "And everyone knows the old saying. Too many cooks spoil the—"

"Salad!" Allie shouted.

Everyone started laughing all over again.

"Well, I think there's only one thing left to do," Stephanie said. She walked over to the telephone and dialed.

"Hello, Luigi's?" she said. "We'd like an order delivered, please!"

Darcy's parents laughed so hard, they had tears streaming down their cheeks. Mr. and Mrs. Taylor had to hold their sides. It was the fifth time that night that Darcy had told the salad-burning story. It was after dinner. Everyone had finished their ziti and eggplant Parmesan from Luigi's. Now they were gathered in the living room.

"I have a feeling I'm never going to hear the end of this story," Stephanie said. "The Day Stephanie

Tanner Burned the Salad—it's going to hang over my head forever."

"Not forever, Steph," Darcy promised. "Just until I get tired of hearing it!"

Stephanie stood up. "Listen, everybody, I have an announcement to make!" Stephanie cleared her throat.

"Well," she went on, "due to circumstances beyond my control, I am hereby announcing the end to Tanner's Tasties. No more catering. No more biscuits, or lamb chops, or mashed potatoes ... and, especially, no more ziti! In fact, I may never cook anything again for as long as I live!"

Everyone laughed.

"I mean it!" Stephanie insisted. "And I'm not going back into that kitchen for at least a month. I'll be happy if I never have to see that room again!"

The front door opened. Jesse and Becky hurried into the house. Becky had a blindfold around her eyes.

"So, Becky, as the perfect ending to your special anniversary day," Jesse said loudly, "I'd like you to get ready for the most romantic anniversary dinner ever!" He winked at Stephanie. "Is it all ready?" he whispered.

Stephanie stared at him blankly. Then it hit her:

She was supposed to make that romantic Japanese anniversary dinner!

Stephanie gasped. "Oh, Uncle Jesse!" she exclaimed. "I totally forgot!"

"Who's that, Jess?" Becky asked from the doorway. "Is that Stephanie? Where are we? I thought we were going to Fujimoto's."

"Just a minute, my little anniversary girl," Jesse said sweetly. Then he spun around to Stephanie. "Stephanie," he growled through clenched teeth, "how could you forget? We planned this days ago! You promised to help me out!"

Stephanie didn't know what to say. In all the cooking confusion, she'd completely forgotten about the dinner—again! "I . . . I . . . uh . . ."

Jesse was fuming. "Hang on just a sec, Becky, sweetie," he cooed. "There's just one small tiny problem."

Stephanie handed him her last six dollars. "Take this, Uncle Jesse," she said.

Jesse stared at the money. "And what am I supposed to do with this?"

"Um, take Becky out for dinner?" she replied. "I'm sorry there isn't more, but Tanner's Tasties has gone bust. I'm broke. That's all I have left. And I might even owe it to someone already. Maybe even to you!"

Jesse's expression softened. "Oh, Steph," he said. "I didn't mean to get all bent out of shape. It's my fault for not making those reservations weeks ago, when Becky asked me to. Don't worry. I'll think of something to do."

"Maybe we can help," Allie's mother suddenly said.

"Jesse, who is that? Where are we?" Becky called from the doorway. She was starting to sound a little impatient, Stephanie thought.

"In a minute, sweets!" Jesse called back to her.

"Why don't we all go to the kitchen and cook you an anniversary dinner?" Allie's mother suggested.

"That's a great idea!" Darcy's father said.

"And I know just the thing," Danny added. "I have two steaks in the freezer."

Stephanie's eyes widened. "That's a great idea!" she said.

"I told you," Danny said. "All you have to do is ask for help."

Stephanie breathed a sigh of relief. "Thanks, everyone."

"Don't mention it, Stephanie," Allie's father said. "It will be fun!"

"And we can set the table all nice and romantic and stuff," Darcy said excitedly.

"Uncle Jesse?" Stephanie asked. "Will that be okay with you?"

Jesse smiled. "Definitely!" he said. "But only if you make those amazing mashed potatoes!"

Everyone looked at Stephanie.

"Cook again?" she asked. "After I've sworn off cooking forever?" She gazed around at everybody.

She grabbed her apron and tied it around her waist.

"One *last* batch of Chef Steph's Tasty Tanner Taters!" she exclaimed. "Coming right up!"

D.J. aimed the video camera at Jesse and Becky feasting on steak and potatoes in the kitchen.

"That's enough video movies, all right, Deej?" Stephanie asked. D.J. nodded and turned off the camera. She followed Stephanie into the living room. Everyone else was collapsed on the couch and chairs, resting from their emergency cooking.

"Well, Aunt Becky and Uncle Jesse love their anniversary surprise dinner," Stephanie reported. "Thanks, everyone. But before I relax, just let me make one hundred percent sure that nothing else could go wrong right now. Do I owe anybody a dinner or anything?"

Nobody spoke.

"Lunch?" she asked.

No answer.

"Breakfast? Birthday parties? Card games? Anniversary dinners? Anything?"

Danny laughed. "No, Steph. You can relax. At least until we figure out your final budget."

Stephanie cringed. Then she remembered something else. After their romantic dinner, everyone would be giving Uncle Jesse and Aunt Becky their anniversary gifts. Her dad and D.J. and Joey had gotten together to get those tickets to a show. Michelle and Nicky and Alex had worked together on that collage. And she, Stephanie Tanner, had nothing—yet. No way could she afford a CD player now!

She'd have to make it up to Uncle Jesse and Aunt Becky with something less . . . extravagant. She could baby-sit Alex and Nicky while they went out, or something. Anything. And the next time a gift-giving occasion came up, she'd remember to take better advantage of good old Tanner teamwork!

Stephanie sank into the sofa. The nightmare was finally over. Except for one last problem.

She turned to D.J.

"I still feel bad for you, Deej," she said. "I ruined your whole economics project."

"No problem, Steph!" D.J. said calmly.

"You mean you're not mad?" Stephanie asked.

D.J. shook her head. "Nope. I just made one tiny, minor adjustment to my project."

"An adjustment?"

"Yup. I changed the topic!" D.J. explained.

Stephanie wrinkled her nose. "You did? To what?" she asked.

D.J. grinned. "Business failures," she said. "I'm calling my report, 'What *Not* to Do When Starting Your Own Business'!"

CLUB STEPHANIE WANTS YOU!

Have Your Name Included in the Upcoming Club Stephanie Books as a Member of Club Stephanie!

FIRST PRIZE

Not only do YOU get to be a MEMBER of Club Stephanie—you also get a Club Stephanie CHARM BRACELET with your name engraved on it—just like the other members of Club Steph!

All you need to do is answer the question:

"Why is Club Stephanie more fun than the Flamingoes?"

Stephanie has been trying to get even with the Flamingoes. With *you* in Club Stephanie, she'll be sure to have the coolest club in school!

Read all about Stephanie's relationship with the Flamingoes in The Full House™: Stephanie Books: Phone Call From a Flamingo and Getting Even With the Flamingoes!

OFFICIAL RULES:
No purchase necessary. If you would like your entry to be considered for the "Club Stephanie" contest, please submit an essay no longer than 75 words. Please send with it your name, age, mailing address and your parent's signature saying it is OK to use your name and story idea to: Pocket Books, Club Stephanie Contest 13th fl, 1230 Avenue of the Americas, New York, NY 10020. One entry per person. Signed submissions constitute permission to use name in the Club Stephanie series. Submission does not guarantee use. Incomplete submissions and submissions received after December 1, 1996, will not be considered. Not responsible for lost, damaged or misdirected mail. No materials will be returned. Void in Puerto Rico and the province of Quebec and where prohibited. All entries will be judged on the basis of originality. All decisions by a qualified panel of judges are final. Pocket Books reserves the right to use the winning name. Winner's parent or legal guardian must execute and return an Affidavit of Eligibility and Liability/Publicity Release within 15 days of notification attempt or an alternate winner will be selected. Winner grants to Pocket Books the right to use his or her name and entry for any advertising, promotion, and publicity purposes without further compensation to or permission from the winner, except where prohibited by law. You must be a U.S. or Canadian (excluding the province of Quebec) resident aged 16 or younger as of 12/1/96. Sole compensation for winning entry will be the inclusion of winner's name in the Club Stephanie series and a 14 karat gold-plated charm bracelet (approximate retail value $25.00). Five second place inclusion of winners will receive one poster autographed by Jodi Sweetin (approximate value $10.00). Twenty-five third place winning-entries will receive one copy of the first *Full House™ Club Stephanie* book available in June 1997 (approximate retail value $3.99). Employees, suppliers, and affiliates of Viacom Inc. and their families are not eligible to participate.